Void Blac[k]

WITHDRAWN

ALSO BY COREY J. WHITE

Killing Gravity

VOID BLACK SHADOW

COREY J. WHITE

A TOM DOHERTY ASSOCIATES BOOK

NEW YORK

This is a work of fiction. All of the characters, organizations, and events portrayed in this novella are either products of the author's imagination or are used fictitiously.

Cover illustration by Tommy Arnold
Cover design by Christine Foltzer

Edited by Carl Engle-Laird

A Tor.com Book
Published by Tom Doherty Associates
175 Fifth Avenue
New York, NY 10010

www.tor.com

Tor® is a registered trademark of
Macmillan Publishing Group, LLC.

ISBN 978-0-7653-9692-1 (ebook)
ISBN 978-0-7653-9693-8 (trade paperback)

First Edition: March 2018

For Chelsea

Void Black Shadow

CHAPTER ONE

The pain is sharp, like needles pricking the flesh of my thigh. I push Ocho down firmly, forcing my cat-thing familiar to lie in my lap and stop kneading me. I scratch behind her ear and within seconds she's purring.

"Alright, Pale; let's try that again."

The boy nods, somber look on his face like this might be life or death. Maybe one day it will be, but right now it's just me throwing chunks of plastic at him.

I take a cube of plastic for the fabricator and toss it fast at Pale's belly. He sweeps his arm and forms a psychic barrier, knocking the block into the wall.

"Good," I say.

I'm cross-legged on the floor with Ocho; Pale stands at the far end of the room. The scars that wreath his skull have started to fade—the white lines barely visible against his white skin. I keep his head shaved, because if he can get a grip on the hairs he pulls them out. I guess it's a stress response, and I can't really blame the kid for being messed up after four years sealed in a metal box. MEPHISTO couldn't trust the psychic boys with autonomy, so they kept them catatonic and ran a surge of current through them to produce psychic blasts on command.

He's looking better than he did when I pulled him out of that weapon platform, but he's still too skinny, his power still lacking in nuance.

I throw another cube, faster and a bit higher, and he knocks it to the other side of the room with a grunt, moving his left hand this time to direct his power.

I'm trying to teach him some of the things the MEPHISTO doctors drilled into me when I was a child: controlling psychic intent through physical movement and vocalization, and using your abilities for defense as well as attack. I'm leaving out the bits where they isolated us from friends and family, starved us and experimented on us, the hypnotic commands, the mind games . . .

"Here's an easy one," I say, but pelt the plastic at his face as hard as I can.

Pale flinches, squeals, and instead of forming a barrier he reverts to the kid in the box, responding to stimulus with violence. His attack sends the cube rocketing over my head, but I ignore it and neutralize the blast itself, catching it and crushing it down to a vibration in the bones of my hand. He's already put a couple of dents in the walls of the *Mouse*—don't need him adding any more. The cube bounces off the wall behind me and hits the ground with a loud clatter. The noise scares Ocho out of my lap, and she leaves fresh punctures in my skin.

"Fuck," I whisper, and Pale starts crying. "No, not you," I say, then I stand and go over to the boy, resting a hand on his shoulder. "Don't worry about it, okay?"

He throws his arms around my waist and I pat him on the head while he sniffles.

"Mars?" Waren's artificial voice comes from the speakers hidden somewhere overhead. Technically the *Mouse* is his ship, but the AI acts like I'm in charge, even though—or maybe *because*—I let him go untethered.

"Yes, Waren?"

"Squid would like to see you aboard the *Nova*."

"Tell them I'll be right over." I make a kiss sound and Ocho runs up my body and deposits herself on my shoulder. "You want to come with me?" I ask Pale.

"Okay," he whispers. He releases my waist, wipes his nose on the sleeve of his shirt, and clasps onto my hand, smiling.

He's a sweet kid, but it's still weird having someone that looks up to me, that wants to be around me. Then again, we are cut from the same cloth, and we've got the matching skull scars to prove it.

I walk to the air lock with my two charges and open both doors, revealing the largely empty cargo hold of the *Nova*.

The *Nova* is a crusher and tug, the sole ship in Squid's scavenging business; though they haven't really had much time to scavenge since I came along. *Sorry, Squid.*

"Einri?" I say loudly, my voice echoing in the massive space. "Where can I find Squid?"

"Captain Squid is in the cockpit," the *Nova*'s AI says, its voice flat, sans voice modulation.

"Thanks."

We make our way through the few scavenged ships and hunks of scrap in the hold, and pass by the living quarters. Winding in and out of the corridors, we reach the mess hall where Trix is tinkering with her exoskeleton, its parts laid out on the dining table.

"Hey, Trix," I say.

She looks at me, then diverts her glance to Pale. "Hi, little man."

He waves with his free hand, and Trix gets back to work. Since we lost Mookie, she's let her crew-cut grow out, and the dark circles beneath her eyes tell me she's barely been sleeping. Her exoskeleton and weapons, though? They've never been so well maintained.

Mookie went AWOL from the imperial military when he met Trix, and that came back to bite him in the ass—thanks to me. After they caught Squid's crew to try and bait me, MEPHISTO sent Mookie away to be court-martialed. Trix has hardly spoken to me since. I don't blame her.

When Pale and I reach the cockpit, Squid is leaning against the viewscreen, wearing a charcoal suit jacket with sharp shoulders and a fine lapel, and loose-fitting pants long enough to pool at their bare feet. Ocho jumps down from my shoulder and trots over to Squid; they turn away from the viewscreen and crouch down to pat Ocho. "How are you, Mars?" they ask.

Guilty? Pissed off? Anxious? I don't know, but I'll feel better when we have Mookie back. "Good," is all I say, saving Squid the hassle of hearing my uncertainties. "Just been training this guy."

"I didn't interrupt, did I?" they ask.

I pick Pale up with a groan and drop him into the pilot's seat. "Nah, we were finished."

"How is it going?" Squid asks, aiming the question at Pale, but he only shrugs in response.

"Slowly," I say. "What did you want to see me for?"

"We're almost there," Squid says; "come have a look." They stand and face the viewscreen, pressing their long fingers against the glass. "There," they say, magnifying a square of the void beyond.

Lekaplica stands out against the darkness, jagged edges jutting out at random.

"How have I not heard of this place before now?" Squid asks.

Two cruisers form the main structure of Lekaplica, fused together top-to-top so they mirror each other. A carrier and countless frigates are attached outboard, like mushrooms sprouting from shit. All told, it has almost as much living space as Aylett Station, but the makeshift structure is notoriously hard to navigate.

"Does that place look like it was put together by professional scavengers?"

Squid chuckles and a flush of pale blue glides across their cheeks. "No, I guess not."

The station is in orbit around a neutron star—the only object of note left in the system after the sun went supernova millions of years back. As far as I know, the system doesn't even have a name. The stackheads chose it because it's an underutilized node in the Trystero network, leaving plenty of spare bandwidth for them to fill with their endless streams of data.

"Transmission incoming," Einri says.

"Patch it through."

"*Nova* crew: please state your name, and your business at Lekaplica." They sound like an AI without a voice mod, but more likely it's a person who wishes they were a machine.

"Lekaplica, this is Mariam Xi." I let that hang in the air for a few seconds. If anyone besides MEPHISTO knows what I did to Briggs's fleet, it's these intel-hunting, data-hoarding weirdos. "I'm here to see a friend: Miguel Guano."

. . .

I walk into Modem, the main bar in Lekaplica's transit hub. The place is packed wall-to-wall with stack-heads—singularity zealots with skulls packed full of augmentations, storing everything they see and hear in the hope of one day digitizing their full consciousness. There's a constant din of chatter: half conversation, half "internal" monologue spoken out loud.

"I'm pretty sure I've had nightmares that started out like this," I say to no one in particular. Ocho must agree, because she makes a low *mraow* and slips off my shoulder to hide in the hood of my cloak.

"Miguel!" I yell it loud and for a split second the bar goes quiet, my voice imprinted into the endless storage of every patron.

I see movement at the bar—Miguel waving—and push forward.

"Hey," I say, as I sidle up beside him.

"Hey, Mars. Good to see you still in one piece," he says. Then in his "inside" voice, *"Did she really destroy a whole fleet single-handed? Shit is crazy."*

"Yes, Miguel, I really did. And since you've brought

me all the way out to the ass-end of nowhere, the least you could do is talk *to* me, not about me."

"Eh, sorry, chica."

"Why aren't you at Aylett, anyway?"

Miguel shrugs. "Didn't want to risk showing my face there after I helped you out. Besides, it's good to be around other stackheads, y'know?"

"I really don't," I say deadpan. "You got what I need? You found out where they're keeping Mookie?"

He doesn't so much shake his head as tip it from side to side.

"Then why am I here, Miguel?"

"Listen; it ain't that easy—we're talking military records, imperial data encryption. But I got you the next best thing."

He grins, and I can tell he's going to make me ask, so I do. "What?"

"The location of MEPHISTO's Data Storage Facility. *All* their records; not just prisoner transfer, but everything they've got about you, about the program, about the other women like you."

It takes me a second to process that.

"Fuck." The word falls from my lips, and Miguel's grin stretches even further. "How much?" I ask.

"*This could be the haul of the decade. Top secret data delivered to me by a void-damned space witch.* How about this: no charge for the intel, but whatever data you can scrape off their servers you forward on to me?"

"Deal," I say, because really, it's too easy to agree now and change my mind later; it's not like *I'm* speaking my thoughts out loud.

He slips a shard across the bar, spreading a ring of condensation over the black glass counter. "Everything you need—just promise me you'll be careful."

"Shit, Miguel, you're worried about me, and you haven't made even one sleazy pass at me: what happened to you?"

"That was only ever in jest, Mariam; I apologize," he says. Then, *"Truth is, I'm scared shitless now."*

I smile at that, slap Miguel on the shoulder, and make my way out of the bar, pushing through the muttering din.

CHAPTER TWO

All around me is black: that impossible nonspace inside of a wormhole. My chest rises and falls inside my space suit as I sit on the hull of the *Mouse* and stare at the hidden infrastructure of the galaxy itself.

"Heart rate is spiking," Squid says, their voice coming through my earpiece from the cockpit. "Are you sure you're okay out there?"

"I'm fine, Squid." My heart's thudding hard in my chest, but that's normal. Staring into the abyss, I *should* be terrified, but honestly, all I can think about is where we're heading.

Ocho squirms inside my suit and climbs into my helmet. She looks out, then turns to face me and makes an annoyed-sounding *maow*.

"You're the one who wanted to come outside with me."

She *maow*s again, and crawls over my shoulder to return to the hood of the cloak I wore under my suit for her sake.

"Coordinates are locked in," Waren says, voice coming

directly from inside the comms system rather than through it, too clean, too close.

"I'm ready," I say.

Squid sounds calm as ever when they give the order: "Hit it."

We shunt through space-time; wide swathes of flat color hang pixelated, then begin to crystallize. As clarity seeps in I see the planet Miyuki, its frozen surface glittering like a bed of precious stones.

"It's beautiful," Squid says over comms. They aren't wrong.

There's a small fleet in orbit around the ice planet, drifting serenely in the void—three frigates surrounded by a swarm of fighters.

As Waren brings us closer, the defense fleet rallies, exhausts glowing bright as starshine as they turn to face the *Mouse*.

"They've seen us," I say.

"You need to deal with them quickly, Mars," Squid says.

"On it. Waren, keep the ship steady for me."

"I'll do my best," he says.

"That's all I ask."

The frigates loose a volley of missiles that streak through the space between us. I reach with my fingers stretched open, spreading my thoughts like a net. I grab hold of the projectiles and fling them back at the fleet. Explosions bubble in vacuum, fighters shatter into fields of floating detritus. One of the frigates lists to the side and tumbles toward Miyuki.

I grab the other two frigates, clench both fists, and feel the ships crumble, hardened chassis resisting for a short moment before the vehicles collapse.

The remaining fighters move in formation, speeding closer. Before I can crush them, the *Mouse* rotates hard to starboard and I'm thrown off the hull. I jolt to a sharp stop at the end of the polyplastic tether.

My mouth opens, abuse for Waren forming on my tongue, but I shut it when a white-hot blast of plasma from the planet's surface streaks past. My helmet darkens in response and the Head-Up Display flashes heat proximity warnings.

"Good flying," I say, winding the tether around my arm and pulling closer to the hull. With my other hand I grab three of the fighters and hurl them; they spin out of control, colliding with the rest of the wing. I reach out wide again, take hold of the ships, and crush. A sound builds in the back of my throat, the only noise in the silence of the void, as one by one the small crafts explode and compact into solid spheres orbited by specks of shrapnel.

Another blast of cannon fire burns toward us from below, and I hold tight as Waren strafes the *Mouse* out of the way.

"I don't know how many more of those I can dodge, Mars," Waren says flatly.

"I can't crush the cannons 'til I know where they are."

"We need to get down there," Squid says, "quickly."

Waren zags to port and my arm throbs as I strain to hold the tether tight.

"Mars, we're about to hit the atmosphere," Squid says.

I start chanting "Fuck fuck fuck" as I unclip the tether and clamber across the hull, gripping handholds as the ship thrashes beneath me like a wild beast.

I swing into the open air lock and punch the controls, then listen to the *thu-thump* of my heart as I wait for the air lock to cycle. When the light over the interior door turns green I duck through the opening and spot Pale. He's strapped to the wall, dressed in a gray space suit too large for him, eyes barely visible over the lip of the helmet.

The ship shudders with an echoing *dhoozh*, and running lights switch from white to red: we just lost atmosphere. I cross the ready-room and check the clasp on the neck of Pale's suit.

"Wait here; keep your helmet on and don't undo these straps, no matter what." His eyes are stuck fast to me, but slowly he nods. His face is blank and I can't tell if it's catatonic terror or simple serenity. He's not much for vox at the best of times, so I don't bother asking.

"We're gonna be okay," I say. I leave him and head for the cockpit.

The floor pitches beneath me. I'm tossed forward, but break my fall with a little telekinetic push. I cut Pale out of the comms circuit and say, "What the fuck is happening?"

"I need you up here now, Mars. We have multiple hull breaches, and we just lost power to the engines," Squid says. "Waren still has thrusters, but that won't be enough to stop us crashing into the planet's surface."

"I'm on my way. Trix, get to the ready-room and wait with Pale."

"Already moving," she says, rounding the corner to head back the way I came. She's wearing her red and black exoskeleton over her space suit, with a hefty-looking lasrifle clipped to the exo's frame. The ship shakes again, but the gyroscopes in Trix's exoskeleton keep her steady while I slam into the wall. I stay there hugging it so Trix's artificially broad frame can push past me.

I keep rushing for the cockpit, progress stunted by the ragged rhythm of the *Mouse* falling down and apart. I pass a viewport and glance outside. The sight is split between void-black and the blue-white of Miyuki's atmosphere, with the glowing orange re-entry burn fluttering past.

When I reach it, the cockpit door slides open for me and I find Squid in the pilot's seat, face slack as they interface with the *Mouse* via skullstack pilot augmentations.

"Squid, I'm here now. I need you to open the blast shield."

They don't say anything, but the shield slides away, revealing a wide stretch of Miyuki's endless white plains.

Puffs of smoke billow as the surface cannons unleash another volley. I grab the back of the pilot seat and, with my other hand, scatter the incoming plasma: balls of superheated matter roiling like living things within my grasp.

"Was that you?" Squid asks, voice coming through comms while their mouth stays static.

"Yes," I yell as I brush the next attack aside. My eyes struggle to focus as the ship shudders against the friction of re-entry.

"If you keep that up we might just make it," Squid says.

There's a squirming between my shoulder blades and Ocho *maow*s hopelessly. I ignore her and stagger from behind the pilot's seat over to the front viewport and lean with both palms flat against the void-proof glass.

"We've lost the last of the thrusters," Waren says, with artificial calm. "We are now in free fall."

What I wouldn't give for an AI's lack of fear right now.

Ocho's latest incarnation is still only juvenile, so she

doesn't hinder my view too badly when she maneuvers into the helmet of my suit. She stares down at the rapidly approaching surface and makes a curious-sounding trill.

"Don't worry, little one: it'll take more than gravity to do us in," I say. Ocho stays in my helmet, with her tail flicking my cheek and a paw pressed against the glass like she's mimicking me.

We're close enough now that I can see the plasma cannons: matte-white shapes on the planet's crystalline surface. In the distance a tall stack rises from a melted patch of snow, the ground almost black beneath all that white. I inhale deep, focus on the cannons, and strike. Masses of snow leap into the sky, forming temporary clouds that clump, scatter, and fall back to the ground. When it settles, huge indentations mar the ice, like some cosmic god is having a fistfight with the planet.

I concentrate on the palm of each hand, drawing strength from every part of my mind. My fingers are splayed on the viewport, digits touching the surface of Miyuki and pushing, slowing our descent as my throat burns and my ears fill with the sound of my shouting.

My eyes sting, lids forced open so I can see; see the looming planet and our fate if I don't stop this fall.

The re-entry burn stops, but the ground is still coming up fast, too fast.

I reach down deep, deeper still, to that reservoir in the furthest part of myself.

Arm muscles burn as I push against the force of a whole planet, push against this falling gravity. The shout becomes a scream and the planet a tear-blurred field of white.

The *Mouse* creaks loudly, metal twisting as I adjust our trajectory. I picture a stone skipping across water and lift the ship's fore; atmosphere shifts around us and we hurtle forward, still rushing at the ground.

"Squid! Get out of here! Go back to the others."

"No!" they yell. "There's no time!"

They're right.

I form the largest barrier I can and hold it in front of the *Mouse*. I watch the ground fly up to meet us as the planet punches back.

CHAPTER THREE

Black. White flashes, tumbling.

Hands aching, fingers clawed in effort.

Mind tingling, singing. *Throb*.

Lungs frozen.

Black, white, black; pain jolts through my whole body as we strike ground, stomach lurches as we rocket forward. Again. Again. We slow, veer sideways, stop.

My hands relax inside their gauntlets, and there's heavy panting inside my helmet. The noise recedes down a black tunnel and darkness returns.

. . .

I come to slowly, with Ocho patting my lips with a paw; I groan and turn my head to escape her prodding. I cough and frozen air burns my lungs. Fragments of shattered helmet glass in my cheek. I unfasten the helmet and drop it to the floor; the warm blood on my face turns cold as the wind of Miyuki pushes through fissures in the *Mouse*'s hull.

I grab Ocho around the belly and find a wet patch of blood on her side. I part the fur, fingers probing for a wound, but there's nothing there.

Oh good; it's only my blood.

Ocho rubs her chin on my hand. I pull the hood of my cloak out from my suit and lift it over my head. I put Ocho on my shoulder, and she crawls into the raised hood and lies down, wrapping herself around the back of my neck.

Squid hangs forward against the chair restraints, forehead touching the glass of their helmet. I crouch in front of them and tap on the glass. "Squid," I say firmly.

Their eyelids flutter, open wide, close, then open again. The chromatophores beneath their skin pulsate green. I open the clasp at the neck of their suit and lift the helmet off.

"Squid, are you okay?"

They twist in the seat, then retch and vomit. They wipe their mouth on the padded sleeve of their space suit and look at me. "That's not the worst landing I've ever experienced, but it *is* close." Squid manages a weak smile, and I stand and help them to their feet. They sway for a moment. "We need to check on the others."

"Wait, I've got to get Waren."

"Alright," Squid says, nodding. "I'll burst a message to Einri, tell it to follow and wait in orbit for us."

I unlock the recessed panel on the rear wall of the cockpit, revealing a metal handle. I twist it and a gray cylinder emerges with a hiss of escaping coolant gases. The AI's brain is dense, small but heavy. Blinking lights down one side tell me it's still operational. I clip it to my suit. "Okay, now we can go."

Squid leads us through the crumpled corridors of the ship while electrical fires fill the air with acrid smoke. When we reach the air lock, the inner door is open. Trix stands by the shattered exterior door, lasrifle raised to her shoulder, looking through her scope at the tundra beyond.

"Hear that?" she asks.

Beneath the sound of the ship settling in its icy grave and the sparking of its electrical systems, there's a low, steady rumble.

"What is it?" Squid says.

"Scrap shower," I say, without needing to look. "The ships I wrecked drifting into the planet's gravity well."

I go unstrap Pale from the wall. A bright gash of glare bounces off his helmet and into my eyes. I block the light so I can see properly, and the look on his face is ecstatic. Is this his first time seeing ice and snow? *Shit, is it his first time on a planet?*

"You okay?" I ask.

He nods.

"We have to get moving," Squid says.

I use my mind to push open the broken fragments of door. The light is blinding at first, and I blink to clear the floating spots from my vision. Snow crunches beneath my feet as I step outside; after a moment the others emerge behind me.

The sky is a cloudless dirty gray, cut with lines of orange-red as wreckage tumbles into the atmosphere. At this distance, all those pieces of MEPHISTO ships look like they're moving slow, like the chunks of debris aren't quickly approaching terminal velocity as they hurtle toward the surface.

"We have company," Squid says.

I follow their pointed finger: three white armored personnel carriers hover across the ice toward us, empty air shimmering beneath them.

I raise a hand but Trix yells, "Wait."

"What?"

"We could use one of those."

"Fuck," I say, because she's right and I would've just trashed them all. *Don't get carried away, Mars.* "Squid, you and Pale stay behind us."

Squid takes Pale's hand and they move back, standing in the mouth of my broken ship—Waren's broken ship.

I look to Trix and she nods, raising her rifle.

I reach out and grab the APC on the right, then toss it

high into the air. It crashes into the ground with a crunch and I smash it flat. I lash out at the one on the left, punching it so hard it flips end over end and crashes into the ice, skidding on its roof before it comes to a halt.

The third APC pivots without slowing, gliding at me and Trix while the two large doors on its side open. It stops dead twenty meters away, inertia launching eight soldiers clad in thick, insulated outfits onto the snow—MEPHISTO black and maroon like a bruise on Miyuki's surface.

The soldiers hit the ground without slowing, their legs churning snow behind them as they run with fluid grace, levelling their weapons at us: bullpup ballistic carbines. They fire short, controlled bursts, but I raise a psychic wall; bullets thud into the shield like rain falling on my mind, then drop into the snow. I grab hold of the guns and tear them from the soldiers' hands, but even that doesn't slow them.

Trix snaps off a shot with her lasrifle and a grunt goes down. I toss three aside, but they land, roll, and get back to their feet in a single movement. I focus on the one closest to me, lift him into the air and clench my fist, but his rib cage holds. *What the hell?* I grunt loud and crush again, too hard this time, and blood explodes across the snow.

I drop the carcass and another soldier leaps over the

body, drawing his sidearm. With one hand I grab his legs, with the other his chest, and I tear him in half, flinging the two pieces aside.

There's a scream behind me.

I spin around: one of the soldiers is almost on Squid and Pale. Before I can react, Pale shrieks again and the soldier is thrown back, striking the ground hard with their chest split open like a bloody maw. Pale sways on his feet for a second, and Squid catches him before he falls, lowering him to the ground as the boy shakes and spasms.

I turn back and another two soldiers have fallen to Trix's lasrifle. The last three rush at her in concert. I grab hold and crush them hard and fast, their mangled corpses smacking wetly as they hit the ground.

I approach Trix and put a hand on one of the steel struts of her exoskeleton. "You good?"

She nods, breath fogging the inside of her helmet as she pants.

I walk over to one of the soldiers that Trix killed. I open his jacket and smell laser-cooked meat; one scent I'd hoped to never come across again. The charred flesh parts to reveal matte metal where his ribs should be. His skin is adorned with hexagonal scarring running across his chest and up his neck—only his face is clear.

Ocho pokes her head out of my hood and lifts her nose into the air.

"No," I say, and she *mraows* sadly as I strip the jacket off the dead soldier.

I take the coat to Squid and they wrap it around Pale.

"Trix, come take a look," I say. She sighs loudly to let me know I'm inconveniencing her, but follows me back to the half-naked corpse. "You seen anything like this before?" I ask.

Trix bends down and inspects the body. After a few seconds she shakes her head. "No. Back in my mercenary days I saw MEPHISTO troops with some brutal augs, but never anything so, I don't know, subtle."

I nod, because that's exactly the word for it—*subtle*. Cyborg supersoldiers that can hide in plain sight. Sneak them onto planets where imperial forces aren't usually welcome, build up slowly, then stage a *coup*. Local authorities would have no idea what was hiding in their midst.

When we get back to Squid and Pale, he's lying in Squid's lap, staring up at the sky; what little color he normally has has completely drained from his skin.

Leaning over the boy, Trix pinches Pale's cheek and he smiles. "You scared us, guy."

Now the adrenaline has drained from my system, I start to shiver. My nose burns in the cold and I grab my hood at my throat and pull it closed as best I can.

"We need to get moving," Squid says.

Trix picks Pale up and carries him to the APC, step-ping over twisted bodies, bones breaking through skin and blood turning to ice. She lays him across three of the seats and turns to Squid. "Which way?"

I shield my eyes and scan the horizon. "There," I say, pointing. The tall black stacks I saw during our descent are barely visible over a distant hill.

Squid nods, then looks to the sky, as overhead the sound of thunder grows—shrapnel descending. "Let's go."

We climb into the APC, and Squid takes the driver's seat. They shift into gear and the vehicle lifts off the ground with a steady hum. As we turn around, I take one last look at the wreck of the *Mouse*.

"Sorry, Waren," I say under my breath, patting the core that still hangs from my suit.

I drop my hood and grab Ocho. Her fur is puffed up, but she's still shivering. I put her inside my suit and zip it up so only her head is showing. She half closes her eyes in appreciation and starts to purr.

The rumbling in the sky grows louder, and there's a deafening *boom* as a colossal piece of former-frigate strikes the ice behind us.

"Hang on!" Squid yells over their shoulder, and we jolt back as they hit the acceleration hard.

Billowing black smoke streaks the sky as the burning

wreckage plummets down. All those broken ships, falling like snow. I try not to think about how many people I killed just getting us down here, but the only thing that can stop me from counting is to picture Mookie's face. If they hadn't taken him, we wouldn't be here.

If Briggs had left me alone, I wouldn't have killed him and every person under his command.

I look over at Pale, craning his neck to watch the sky show of destruction.

"Mars?" he says, his voice barely a squeak.

"Yeah?"

"That was fun." He smiles.

Trix laughs once, but when I look to her, she turns away.

Fun? Fuck. He's too young to realize that mass destruction isn't meant to be fun, that you're not meant to take a life so casually.

He's young; what's my excuse?

CHAPTER FOUR

We pass the crushed and smoking wrecks of the defense cannons on our way to the main facility. Squid slows the APC as we approach, in case more troops are lying in ambush, but there's no resistance.

The facility is a squat structure, made to look taller by the long, wedge-shaped heatsinks that reach up to the firmament. The heat output melts snow in a ten-meter ring around the building, marring the fields of white with a large black moat of sodden dirt.

The massive door off to one side of the building opens automatically. Squid takes us down into the garage and parks the APC near the entry to the facility proper.

"Einri just arrived in orbit with the *Nova*," they say. "It's ready to send the shuttle whenever we need."

"Great," I say, as I step out of the APC and stretch. My breath comes in white plumes, but it's warmer down here in the vehicle lot with the door closed. Not *warm*, just warmer than below-fucking-freezing.

Trix steps down from the APC, exofoot clanging against the ground. "What happened with Pale back there? You were meant to be training him," she says, words thick with venom.

"I'm teaching him to control his powers, but I can't do shit about his fear or trauma."

Squid climbs through to the back of the APC and sits so Pale can rest his head in their lap. Despite his pallor, Pale's eyes are bright and watch us intently as we speak.

"You saw what he did to that soldier; what if that was the hull of the ship he tore apart?"

"Then we might have crashed," I say, sardonically. Ocho shifts between my shoulder blades; she's asleep, unaware of, or unconcerned by, the loud argument happening around her.

"Can we talk about this later?" Squid pours water from a canteen into Pale's mouth.

"He can't help it," I say, ignoring Squid.

"That's exactly the problem."

"Fuck off, Trix; he's just a kid," I say.

Trix sneers, and I half expect her to cross the gap between us, slam me against the hull of the APC, and try and strangle me; you know, that old song and dance. She shakes her head, but stays put. "Doesn't mean he isn't dangerous."

"We don't know what MEPHISTO did to him," Squid says, "but he's unstable, and we need to do something about the seizures."

I nod. "Miguel said all of MEPHISTO's records are here; we'll find what they did to Pale. In the meantime, we should put him to sleep," I say, and at that Trix steps forward. I hold a hand up and say, "Not *permanently*, fuck. If Pale's sedated, he won't freak out; if he doesn't freak out then he won't push his powers too far and hurt himself."

Trix scoffs. "Or us. And we can't keep calling him 'Pale'; it's a descriptor, not a name."

"How does 'Bob' sound?" I say, winking at Pale. "I think he looks like a 'Bob.'"

"Seadation is probably the safest bet, for now," Squid says.

"Fine." Trix grunts, then crouches down, exoframe clanging against the floor. "Strap the kid on then."

Squid and I fasten Pale to the exoskeleton and I zip up his oversized jacket. Trix walks to the exit and Pale smiles as his whole body is swung from side to side with Trix's mechanical gait.

CHAPTER FIVE

Exiting the garage brings us to a bank of elevators. I hit the call button and the nearest door opens, spilling yellowish light across the floor. I let Trix and Squid in first, then follow. The air smells like the inside of a refrig unit—a dank, clinically unclean scent.

A holographic list hangs an inch from the wall, letters refracted off burnished steel: Data Storage, Administration, Garrison, Medical Research.

"Medical first," Squid says, poking a finger into the shimmering lights.

We're already underground, so I expect the elevator to move up, but it descends further beneath Miyuki's frozen surface.

After a minute the elevator slows. A tone chimes and the doors slide open on a wide, empty corridor of white walls. I step out and check the corners, my boots squeaking on the rubbery flooring, gray marbled with streaks of black. The damp odor of the elevator gives way to the scent of antiseptics—a sharp smell that burns clean through my nostrils.

At the far end of the corridor is a set of doors in frosted glass. I move forward and the others follow, the whir of Trix's exo over-loud in the enclosed space.

I press the large button in the center of the door and it splits, revealing a cavernous room bisected by a curtain of clear polyplastic. Hospital beds line one of the walls, each attended by an autodoc, and beyond the transparent veil sit rows of large cages, their walls opaque and darkened by shadows.

I expected more movement in Medical—doctors and nurses doing their rounds, rushing about and barking jargon—but the place is quiet. Most of the autodocs stand dormant; only a few glow with blue-green light.

Directly ahead is the nurse's station, staffed by four personnel in stark white uniforms trimmed with MEPHISTO maroon: two men, a woman, and one other person.

The older of the two men cocks an eyebrow. "Where are the wounded from the fight outside?" he asks as we advance, his deep voice filling the entire space for those few short seconds.

"There are no wounded," Trix says, moving closer.

"No survivors, even," I add.

The man looks confused, and four pairs of eyes sweep over us, scanning Trix's weapon and exo, like *she's* the threat. The nonbinary staffer inhales sharply and puts their arms up; only then do the other three figure out who we are.

"Oh, void," the woman says, raising her arms to match her colleague's stance.

When I reach the counter I lean over to check they aren't hiding any weapons.

"Seeing as there are no wounded to help," Squid says politely, "perhaps you could help us instead?"

"We need something for the kid's seizures." Trix turns so they can see Pale, dangling from her exoskeleton. "Sedatives, tranquilizers, whatever—you're the experts."

The woman nods and lowers her arms. She walks to a large cupboard built into the wall, doors almost seamless but marked with grimy finger smears. She stacks a pile of pillboxes, one atop the other with a flat clap, then she comes back and drops the cartons on the bench, keeping her eyes to the floor the whole time.

"He'll only need half a tablet, once every four hours," she says, stuttering.

Squid removes a pill from one of the packets and breaks it in half, then steps behind Trix. "I need you to take this, Pale, okay?"

The boy nods and swallows the pill with a swig of water from Squid's canteen.

"It's no use," the older man says, "you cannot help the boy."

"Why's that?" I say.

His face is webbed with wrinkles and the side of his head is lined with deep scars in geometric patterns—the same as the soldiers we fought outside. He taps these scars with a finger, then says, "The Legion is endless, and they are coming here. They dispatched reinforcements the moment you killed the elements on the surface. They will be here soon to protect me."

"What makes you so special?" Trix asks.

"They need me, they need my work." The doctor continues, but I'm already headed for the nearest hospital bed.

The autodoc gives me a canned greeting as I approach, though "autovet" might be more accurate: the unconscious patient is a large, shaved primate. My stomach turns at the sight of the needles stuck in its right arm, delivering pain relief, or something else, from two fluid pods. The animal's other arm is splayed open, flesh ending just beneath the elbow, metal bones exposed and glossy beneath the ceiling lights. The forearm is held in a hermetically sealed pod, tiny robotic digits rapidly threading veins, nerves, and muscle into place, knitting flesh onto bone in neat hexagonal segments.

Ocho wriggles out from my jacket and jumps onto the bed, cautiously sniffing the sleeping primate. She turns to look at me and *yaow*s.

"I know," I say, then I pick her up and press her to my shoulder. "What the fuck is *this*?" I say, storming back to the four medical workers now lined up against the wall, restrained by Trix's lasrifle.

"What's over there?" Squid asks.

I shake my head and glare at the older man.

He lifts his chin, but doesn't meet my eyes. Proudly, he says, "That is my work. I develop new limbs, new nervous systems, and new epidermises. My research makes the Legion stronger, faster."

"So you flay helpless animals?"

He opens his mouth to speak, but then closes it. I poke his chest to make him look at me. "You keep saying 'the Legion' like we should know what that means. They're a bunch of cyborgs—so what?"

"They move and fight as one. They are Commander Hamid's forces, but they are greater than her."

Squid catches my eye and nods toward the bed, then goes to inspect the animal.

"If he's telling the truth and they have reinforcements coming, we need to hurry," Trix says.

"Just a minute," I say. Trix glares at me, but I ignore her and push through a slit in the polyplastic wall.

Even with most of the cages sealed, the smell of feces and rotting fruit is thick enough to choke on. Ocho *yaows* again, louder and right beside my ear.

I scratch her chin. "I don't like it either, little one."

One of the plastic cages has a large shadow across its front panel. I key the opacity to clear, and see it's a smaller primate, sleeping crouched in the corner. Green-gray fur covers its body in patches, and bits of metal show through beneath the skin. Both its arms have been replaced with human-sized cyborg limbs, skin stretched and split over the too-large prosthetics. This is what the animals look like after surgery—painfully altered, bloodied, broken.

My eyes burn. I don't cry, but I could. The creature whimpers in its sleep, feet shuffling over the floor of the cage.

I find the master controls and turn all the cages transparent. My breath catches in my throat when I see them, each one wretched and damaged, glinting with steel where there should be flesh.

In the tortured animals I can't help seeing myself, and Ocho, and Pale. I feel the needles and remember the rooms and the doctors and the tests. Even some of the smells are the same—the sickeningly familiar mingling scents of antiseptic, latex gloves, piss, and shit.

There are twenty animals, give or take, each a different sort of primate. One is awake and eyeing me warily—it can't tell that I'm not one of the doctors, it can't know that I'm not one of the people who did this. I grab it and squeeze. A noise builds in my throat as I crush the tiny thing's reinforced ribs, but the growl isn't loud enough to cover its dying yelp.

I open my mind wide enough to take in all the animals, and with a scream loud enough to stir the sleeping ones, I crush them. I do it hard and fast, to make sure they don't suffer, but still I hear a few cry out.

The sharp smell of blood fills my nose as I turn away. I can kill people in the hundreds when I need to, but this? This is different. Is that fucked up? If it is, blame Ocho.

I drop down to my haunches and take Ocho from my shoulder. I hold her tight against my chest; she squirms for a few seconds before stopping to let me pet her.

"I'm sorry, Ocho, I'm sorry," I say, though I'm not sure why.

I exhale slowly until my chest stops rattling, then I return to the others. I stop behind Trix and make sure Pale's asleep: he's seen enough carnage for one day.

I step up to the doctor, close enough to see the fine points of sweat beading on his head and smell the coppery stink of his breath. "That's your work too?"

"The Legion's next generation relies on me perfecting the treatments. The animals suffer, but the results are worth it."

I shake my head and take a step back. I wrap my thoughts around his skull, but I don't bother squeezing the metal cranium. Instead, I yank his head free from the neck; vertebrae crack and pieces of bone burst through mangled flesh.

The doctor's body slumps back and slides down the wall. I drop his head into his lap and red seeps through the material—cohesion leaching blood across the fabric. The younger man screams while the others watch in silence, eyes wide in horror.

"Are you okay?" Trix asks. I'm so surprised by her concern that I don't answer at first, and after a few long seconds have passed, it feels like the moment has too. "I'll kill the others," she says.

"What?" Squid says, sounding incredulous.

"The animals, I mean. So Mars doesn't have to." It's the first time since we lost Mookie that she's treated me like a friend.

"Thank you," I say, staring down at the doctor's corpse but not really seeing it.

She goes to the bed, and her gun whines as it charges. Her shadow stretches across the ceiling, haloed by the bright white of laserfire. There's a sizzle and the autodoc makes a distressed beep. She shoots the doc too and continues to the next occupied bed.

Squid takes a medic bag marked with a white cross from behind the counter, and stashes the rest of Pale's drugs inside.

Trix returns, and before we can talk about the other three workers, before I have to decide how complicit they are in animal torture and experimental surgery, I turn back toward the entrance.

We're leaving them here, faced by the doctor's corpse, and surrounded by the soon-decaying bodies of all those animals.

Hopefully that's punishment enough.

CHAPTER SIX

A heavy silence hangs over the elevator as it lifts us toward Data Storage.

"We're going to get him back," I say, partly to break the quiet, and partly to repay Trix's earlier kindness. I glance over, but her face is impassive beneath the wan yellow light. I can't tell what she's thinking, but after a few long seconds without a response, I continue: "It's my fault, and you hate me, and that's fine, but I won't stop 'til he's safe."

Trix sighs. "You think talking about Mookie will make me forget *why* he's gone?" She shakes her head. "I thought you didn't like to sit around, telling stories and holding hands."

Now it's my turn to sigh. I don't push any further.

The elevator stops, and when the doors part diffuse white light fills the car. Data Storage is the only part of the facility aboveground; the remainder rests beneath the surface of Miyuki the way an iceberg's bulk hides beneath the water. That way, most staff on-site can avoid the freezing conditions outside, while the waste heat from

MEPHISTO's servers is easily offset.

Squid disembarks first and I follow, squinting until my eyes adjust. It's a short, glass-walled corridor that wears a fine coating of crystalline ice. At the far end is an armored steel door marked with security clearance restrictions and dire warnings in four languages.

Squid tries the control panel beside the door: it *boops* an anguished tone and stays closed.

"Could you try knocking, Mars?"

I roll my eyes but laugh. "Yeah, sure."

Squid moves aside, and I use my mind to grab hold of the door, feeling its mass as a single heavy point near the back of my skull. The metal frame screeches and twists as I tear the door off its hinges and yank it free. There's a loud thud when I lower the door to the ground and another when I lean it against the glass wall beside the opening.

"Did you hear that?" Squid asks.

"The door?"

"No, listen."

There's a series of distant, irregular booms. I step over to the southern wall of the corridor and Trix joins me, pounding on the glass with the forearm of her exoskeleton to knock some of the ice loose. She unslings her rifle and looks down the scope, pointing it toward the distant field of wreckage that juts from the snow like so many headstones.

Overhead, a dozen white streaks slice through the sky—more ships coming into orbit, descending fast enough to break the sound barrier on their way to the surface.

"Another fleet incoming," I say.

Trix tracks one of the trails, then hands me the rifle. "Not a fleet—ROTs."

I raise the weapon, straining at first because Trix makes it look so easy. It takes me a few seconds to get one of the objects into focus through the rifle's powerful scope: a Rapid-response Orbital Torpedo—colloquially known as a "drop-pod." Basically the same as the pod that delivered Briggs's envoy to Ergot, but designed to drop soldiers into battle without turning them into meat paste. The ROT is a black cylinder, tapered at both ends and marked with a single stripe of maroon. The air beneath it shimmers, distorted by its engine burning at full-reverse.

The far-off whine of the landing pods lowers in pitch, and they plunge into the snow in quick succession. A pod door blasts open on explosive bolts. At this distance, the soldier that steps out is a few pixels tall, just enough for me to see MEPHISTO colors and the glint of weaponry. The Legion has arrived—just like the doctor promised.

I hand the lasrifle back to Trix and enter Data Storage through the wrecked opening. It's warm inside, a dry heat—like, zero percent humidity—and right away the skin on my face feels like it's flaking. The temperature climbs as I pass the nearest cylindrical server stack, waves of heat emanating off it. There must be a hundred of them—black monoliths lined with flickering lights of inexplicable purpose. It's loud in here surrounded by the machines, countless quiet whirrings combining to form a relentless din. Squid is already walking along the northern wall searching for an open console.

"Trix," I call out, "keep an eye on those troops and let me know when they get close."

I rush to the far end and join Squid's search for a workstation that's already on and aglow with hope.

"Squid, you better get Einri to send the *Nova*'s shuttle down for exfil."

"Already done," they say.

I find a console that's powered up, standby light winking infrequently enough that I almost miss it. I put Ocho down beside the console and she walks into the lightkeys, bringing the interface to life. She complains when I grab her, but then I sit and put her in my lap, and she quickly settles. I find the search function and type *Mookie Healerman*. A green bar fills from left to right, and the console chimes.

It gives me a couple hundred results, each one less relevant than the last, until I'm scrolling past entries for people named "Marky" or "Hillman" and cursing under my breath.

"There's nothing here," I yell.

"What?" Squid says, running over to join me. They lean in over my shoulder. "What name did you use?"

"'Mookie Healerman'?"

Squid looks at the screen and laughs. "He's a medic, and his surname just happens to be 'Healerman'?"

The pieces fall into place, and I say, "He changed his name when he went AWOL."

"Precisely," Squid says. "May I?"

I get out of the seat and hold onto Ocho, then drop her into Squid's lap as they sit down and start to glide their fingers through the keys.

"How's it looking out there?" I yell to Trix.

"About half are heading to the wreckage of the *Mouse*, the rest are marching this way."

Another chime draws my eyes back to the console.

Squid opens the file for Cadwell Amos Moreland and scrolls past his basic details, looking to find out what they've done with him.

"He's alive," Squid says, "being held at a place called Homan Sphere."

Before I need to ask, Squid drills down further into the files. I read over their shoulder, taking it all in. *Homan Sphere*: it's not an official imperial prison, it's not even a military prison—it's MEPHISTO's own facility; a designated black site, beyond-maximum security. The file doesn't say who gets sent there, but from the language used I can guess: traitors, dissenters, anyone with the gall to stand against the empire. I doubt Mookie even got court-martialed before they disappeared him.

I point at the console to where the location coordinates glimmer. "Could you burst them to Einri?" I ask Squid, then I open a link with the AI: "What do you make of these coordinates?"

There's a loud burst of static as Einri's voice curves around from the far side of Miyuki's moon where the *Nova* is hiding. Einri says, "Those coordinates are well beyond the limits of colonized space."

"Fuck," I say, "that's what I thought."

"Mars," Trix yells, "I need you over here!"

"You go," Squid says. "I'll see what I can find about Pale."

I unclip Waren's cylinder from my belt and pass it to Squid.

"Mind Waren's brain for me?"

"Of course," Squid says.

"And while you're in there, could you look for anything on Commander Briggs, the voidwitch program, or my father, Marius Teo?"

"Marius Teo," Squid repeats, nodding.

I turn away and Ocho leaps off Squid's lap to follow me. I scoop her up and put her back beside the console, but she *mraow*s loudly, runs up to sit on my shoulder, and nuzzles my ear.

"Alright, alright," I say. "But you better not get in the way, and you better not fucking die again."

I join Trix in the corridor and she lowers her weapon.

"He's alive," I say. Her face stays blank—no smile, no tears, just the glow of daylight reflected in her eyes.

Out the window, a dozen Legionnaires are approaching, closing on the moat of slush around the facility.

I rest a hand on the glass wall and push outward with my mind. The wall shatters into a hundred razor shards that I hold floating. I spread them aside and step through the opening, my boots sinking into the black mud with a loud squelch. Trix follows, her weapon primed but pointed at the ground.

Seeing us emerge from the building, the Legionnaires rush forward like liquid, flowing into a semicircle with choreographed precision, each one pointing a ballistic carbine at me and Trix.

"This planet is a restricted area," the troops say in unison—even their inflections match. "You are under arrest, by order of their Imperial Highness."

One of the grunts steps forward and pushes back the hood on his jacket, revealing pink geometric scars. I recognize him, I'm sure of it—one of the bodychoppers who stood up for me on Aylett when MEPHISTO came, looking to take me back. He had a pincer for a hand back then, but that's been replaced: a new hand made of metal and fresh gene-fabricated tissue. What else do they replace when they make their Legionnaires? Their names? Their memories? Are they still themselves?

On his own he says, "Come along quietly, or we will use lethal force."

Trix lifts her weapon and shoots him in the chest. The piercing beam of white casts his face in deep shadows for an instant before he collapses to the ground, smoke and blood vapor drifting from the wound.

The other Legionnaires shift slightly, fingers tightening on triggers, but I snatch their weapons away before they can fire. I crush the guns and discard the pieces, then launch my knives of broken glass. Three more Legionnaires go down, clutching at wide red gashes splitting their throats. The rest don't hesitate before rushing forward, drawing blades and laser sidearms.

Trix keeps firing as I lash out hard at the nearest three; they tumble back and others leap at me. I throw one aside and grab hold of two more. Their limbs wheel as they struggle in mid-air, and I squeeze, yelling loud as their reinforced skeletons twist and break. The bodies hit the slick mud underfoot with a wet thud.

The one I tossed aside moves like lightning, and the air is knocked from my lungs as he tackles me to the ground. I twist under him just in time to see Ocho attack, leaving deep scratches across the soldier's scarred neck. She drops to the ground hissing, and before the grunt can react I lift him with one hand. With the other I tear into his stomach—the only soft spot on these cyborgs. I throw him away again, but this time his intestines trail out behind him to splat messily across the ground.

A Legionnaire smacks Trix's gun from her hand, and she grabs hold, lifting him high with the help of her exoskeleton. She punches him in the face with her prosthetic fist until metal skull shows through the red. He's still struggling, while two more soldiers close in behind Trix.

I reach back, remembering the tall, tapered heatsinks that emerge from the facility's roof like spears. I break a dozen of these black metal barbs free, then scan my eyes over the melee, wrists flicking as I launch the spikes at each Legionnaire. The lengths of metal skewer the soldiers with two wet *squicks*—one as they pierce flesh, and the second as they spear into the mud. The soldiers are pinned to the ground like insects on display, except these ones are still squirming against their restraints. They die slowly, limbs going slack, blood bubbling from mouths. I don't know how their hive mind works, but I hope the whole fucking Legion feels that pain.

While I catch my breath, Trix retrieves her lasrifle and points the scope in the direction of the *Mouse*—wreckage still smoldering, but now wearing a thin layer of snow.

"The others are coming this way," she says.

"OK," I say. "Einri, how far out are you?"

"ETA one minute."

"Great, land at the northern side of the building and take off on my command."

"I only take orders from Captain Squid," Einri says.

"I don't have time to argue. Just do it," I say as I stalk back toward the facility.

"What are you planning, Mars?" Trix asks.

I step through the opening in the glass, and over my shoulder I say, "You need to take Pale to the shuttle, Trix; I'll hold them off."

She follows me inside, and I break a panel on the opposite side of the corridor as Einri lands the shuttle. It sits just beyond the ring of dark mud, door open and ramp extended.

Squid joins us in the corridor. "I found everything I could in MEPHISTO's systems," they say.

"Could you just burst the text to me? I don't know if my membank could take the full digital records."

"Done," they say, and a new message icon blinks in my HUD.

"Thank you. Now, go get in the shuttle."

Squid crosses one arm over the other. "What are you planning?"

"I asked the same thing," Trix tells Squid.

Fuck; I've never had a good poker face.

I contemplate repeating the lie that I'm just going to hold the Legion off, but they deserve better. "Where Mookie's being held, we won't be able to just go and break him out; it'll be too dangerous. But if I can get inside . . ."

"No," Trix says. "You don't deserve to make a heroic void-damned sacrifice."

I grab her by the arm of her exo and Squid follows as I walk Trix out of the hallway, toward the shuttle. A cold breeze comes from the north, and even the ambient heat from the server farm isn't enough to stop my teeth from chattering.

"I'm not sacrificing shit," I say. "I'm going to get Mookie out, and I'm going to kill as many people as I have to in the process. This is my fuck-up, so now I'll fix it."

As we near the shuttle's ramp Trix pulls free. "You don't have to do this alone," she says over the hum of the shuttle's engines.

"I put him in this shit, not you; so *go*, Trix."

"She was going to leave him," Squid blurts out. Trix shoots them a glare colder than the wind. "Mars deserves to know," they say.

Trix sighs. "Back on Aylett, I was going to leave, but then they caught us and beat Mookie half to death, and I stayed." She laughs, a sad, broken sort of laugh. "I was bored before you showed up. I was gonna go back to merc-work—even had a meeting lined up."

"Oh, Trix," is all I can manage to say.

"He's out there somewhere, and he doesn't know I was going to leave him, he doesn't know I don't . . .

"I have to be the one that saves him; I owe him that much."

"Listen, Trix; I still don't know how I'm going to get Mookie out of there. I need you on the outside. I need someone hiding near the prison with a ship, ready to swoop in and rescue us when I send out a signal."

"Damn it," Trix says. "Alright."

I scratch Ocho under the chin, then hold her out toward Squid. "Take Ocho and go," I say. Ocho squirms and tries to scratch me with her back legs, but I hold her tight and press her to Squid's shoulder until they get a grip on the little furball.

"Go now; don't make me throw you in there." I see the look on Trix's face, and I can guess how hard it was for her to say all that, but we're running out of time.

Squid starts up the ramp, and when Trix follows I steal a glance at Pale, still in his drug-induced slumber. *Mookie first, then I'll save you too; save you from whatever MEPHISTO did to you.*

I take a moment's respite from the cold inside the corridor. "Einri, you've got to launch the shuttle now and leave me behind."

"Oh," the AI says. "This is what you meant?"

"Yes."

The noise of the shuttle's engines climbs in pitch and volume as it lifts up off the ground. "I understand, ma'am. Good luck." The shuttle hovers for a second, then blasts into the sky.

I walk out the other broken window and face south. The distant Legionnaires grow slowly as they run toward the facility. I figure I've got a couple of minutes before they reach me, so I open the data package Squid sent me.

Briggs's file comes up: compared to what we found on Mookie, it's an encyclopedia. I skip over the start of his career and stop at the point where he was given command over one half of MEPHISTO's research and operations.

I don't see any reference to myself, but there's a whole file on my father—*Marius Teo*, a "brilliant geneticist," and the only researcher to successfully develop telekinetic potential as part of PROJECT SALEM. There's another entry under his name: PROJECT DIANUS. I open that and find schematics for brain augmentations and, scrolling down further, the weapon platform I found Pale trapped inside.

First Teo gave Briggs his brood of voidwitches, but that wasn't enough. Briggs wanted a way to use the boys too, so my father gave him those machines.

I focus my eyes past the text and close the file; the Legionnaires have slowed about a hundred meters away. If they felt what I did to their buddies, they'll be cautious.

I drop to my knees, raise my hands in the air, and form a dome of psychic will just large enough to shield me, in case they decide to kill first and get answers from my corpse.

The soldiers approach warily, weapons trained on my center of mass. When they reach the ring of sludge, a woman steps forward and lowers her weapon. "What is the meaning of this?"

I let out a loud sigh, hoping it sounds like one of exhaustion, rather than impatience. "Are you in charge?" I ask, though her uniform is indistinguishable from the rest.

"No *one* of us is in charge here; we all report to Commander Hamid. I ask again, what is the meaning of this? I will not ask a third time."

"My name is Mars Xi. I'm responsible for the deaths of Commander Briggs and the people under his command.

I also destroyed Miyuki's defense fleet, wiped out the garrison stationed here, and killed your friends," I say, motioning to the dead Legionnaires, arranged in macabre formation across the mud and snow. I drop my head so none of them can see me smirk behind the hair that falls over my face.

"Now that you've lured us here, are you planning to kill us too?" the woman asks.

"I've pushed myself too hard; I'm spent," I lie. "I don't want to die, so I'll come along quietly."

The woman doesn't speak, but the collective mind of the Legion must come to some decision, because one of the troopers stows his gun and unclips a pair of hefty-looking restraints from his belt. He approaches carefully and I bring my shield down before he touches it.

"You better send me to the deepest pit in the fucking galaxy," I say, "or you'll learn what Briggs knew in his final moments."

"And what is that?" the woman who is *not* in charge asks.

"I can't be stopped."

She smiles, and the movement is mimicked on the faces of the other Legionnaires, then something sharp pricks the side of my neck.

Before I can protest, my head swims and I drown in darkness.

CHAPTER SEVEN

I wake to a droning hum, but it takes a few seconds before I'm sure it isn't coming from inside my head. Engine noise. A ship.

My eyelids feel heavy as they flicker. I only get them open with effort.

The door slides open and a young Legionnaire walks in. "Commander Hamid wishes to speak with you," he says, voice authoritative beyond his years.

"Huh? Send 'em in then," I say, fighting my slack mouth to form the words.

I wait for Hamid to walk into my cell, but instead the trooper says, "You must be Mariam." His voice has shifted up a register and softened: a woman's voice coming from his mouth. "Commander Briggs's pride and joy."

I try to laugh, but I barely manage a hoarse bleat from the back of my throat. "Even if I hadn't killed him, I doubt he'd agree with you."

"You were everything he wanted his girls to be. Though I suppose he preferred them a little more . . . malleable." Hamid's wry expression looks wrong on this young man's face, muscles moving in ways they aren't ac-customed to. She continues: "That's why I wanted to see you. You are about to be delivered to a truly awful place, but I can have the Legion divert you if you agree to work for me."

Even if I didn't *want* to go to Homan, the thought that I might join MEPHISTO is as laughable as it is fucking disgusting.

"No deal," I say.

There's a long pause, then the guard's face frowns. Hamid says, "Mariam, I'm trying to help you here." She sighs. "Choose to join me now, or in time we will break you; we will force you to join the Legion."

"You can't break what's already broken," I say.

Apparently Hamid has already stopped listening though, and in his own voice the soldier says, "We're nearly there." He leans down close and there's a sharp pain in my arm. I try to look away, but a restraint collar digs into my neck. I have to watch him pull the blood-steeped needle from my skin. I want to retch, but I swal-low and force myself to breathe, and my head starts to clear.

"A squad will be here shortly to transfer you."

He removes the collar from my neck. I gulp again, but there's still a dull ache where the restraint sat snug at my throat.

The Legionnaire holds the needle up to my face and I pull back. "Your *abilities* will be out of reach until these drugs make their way through your system." He spits the word "abilities" at me. I assume the Legion is pissed that I killed some of its parts, but that's what happens when you bring cyborgs to a space witch fight. "The prison has other ways to keep you in line."

"Are you done?" I say, forcing a smirk. "Let's go already, I'm bored." It takes a few seconds for me to focus on his face, but when I do I see a confused look spread across his features. *That's right—I'm not afraid of your guns or your prison; I chose this. You think I'm your prisoner? You're all dead fucks walking, and I'm a monster in human skin.*

He crouches and unfastens the restraints around my ankles. I stand and feel that woozy tightness as my blood pressure spikes. The Legionnaire studies me with his hand resting on his sidearm. There's a tight tattoo of approaching boots, and he says, "Come along, then." He motions toward the door with a nod.

I step out of the cell and into the hallway; my legs ache, muscles struggling after untold time spent unused. The corridors are packed tightly with MEPHISTO troops—all of them bearing scars that hint at their cyborg skeletons.

Two guards grab me by the arm. The woman barely

comes up to my shoulder, but if anything, her grip is stronger. They perp-walk me down the hall and I hear the others fall in step behind us. As we move through the ship, Legionnaires duck into doorways and alcoves to let us pass, movements all seemingly choreographed, like I'm the only one who skipped rehearsals.

It takes us ten groggy minutes of walking before we reach an interior air lock door marked *Hangar Deck*. I don't recognize the design of the vessel, but from the size of the ship's hangar I'd say it's a carrier.

The hangar bustles with countless Legionnaires in MEPHISTO uniforms. To the left are the external air locks, and far to the right are a collection of shuttles and sleek fighters in their bays. The middle of the deck is taken up with row after row of ROTs. They're suspended from the ceiling on complicated apparatus, hanging over massive doors marked with caution stripes in yellow and black; they're bombs ready to be dropped from space, carrying a cyborg payload.

For a second I think maybe they'll drop me to the prison in one of those pods, but before I can decide if I like that idea the troops corral me to one of the main air lock doors. There's a large viewport to one side, filled with deep black and smudges of color. I blink and my eyes slowly focus; the blur shifts and clears, revealing a planet drenched in sunlight. Its surface is mostly sapphire ocean, but there's a single yellow-green continent run-ning long and thin from one pole to the other, with a scat-tering of islands lost in the immensity of the sea.

"Is that Homan?" I ask, wondering how I'm meant to find Mookie on an entire prison planet, slowly realizing how little I thought this through.

"No," one of the soldiers says. I wait for him to con-tinue, but he stays silent.

"There." One of the others points toward a small brown moon coming into view from behind the planet. It drifts closer in its orbit; flashes of metal line the rock, but I can't see any large structures. "That is Homan Sphere; your new home, and your hell."

A third celestial body comes into view—another moon, pale orange and large enough to dwarf the prison. The three objects shift and dance, overlapping each other on a background of endless void. We're beyond the edge of the empire, civilization somewhere far behind us, and the visible constellations are entirely alien to me. These are the stars of far-off galaxies, impossibly small, infinitely distant.

We're carried nearer, and the rock of Homan's surface fills the viewport; I still don't see any buildings.

"Where's the prison?" I ask.

"You'll see."

We come in, but not to land. We pull up close to a

metal outcropping jutting out like a thumb from a closed fist. An echoing rumble fills the hangar as we dock—an ominous sound, full of dark promise.

For the first time since I let the Legion capture me, I start to wonder if this is a good idea. *It's a bit late for that now, isn't it?*

CHAPTER EIGHT

The ship's air lock twists open, segments disappearing into the hull to reveal a long corridor. Light floods in from the end of the tunnel and refracts off curved walls of galvanized steel, and despite the glowing lines along the floor, the tunnel is dark and I'm blinded by the bright light flooding in at the far end. Turret installations line the ceiling, gun barrels poking into the tunnel like the antennae of curious insects.

I start walking and the boots of the soldiers make a precise beat as they follow. There's no second air lock door at the end of the tunnel, just a heavy barred gate—the prison relying on the air lock of any docked ship, willing to let everyone inside die to decompression rather than give prisoners any hope of escape.

My feet stop at the edge of daylight and, with a grind of machinery, the gate rises. A weapon is jabbed into the small of my back, and one of the voices behind me barks, "Keep moving."

I walk forward and instinctively try to raise a hand to shield my eyes, but my arms are strapped together tight.

Instead I squint until my eyes adjust to the sunlight ...
No, not sunlight, something else.

We're standing on a flat expanse of polycrete. Directly
ahead is a large transparent tube, two meters tall and ex-
tending out of sight in both directions. Behind this tube
are two watchtowers, and beyond them the inside of the
moon's shell curves up above us. A massive forest covers
most of the right hemisphere, broken up by prison compounds and cut into sections by endless lengths of transit tube. The nearest tree line looks close enough to walk
to, but the farthest copse is inverted, pointing "down" toward the other side of the sphere, where a rectangular
stretch of water shimmers. The pond, the trees, *everything*, held in place by centrifugal force, artificial gravity,
or some combination of the two.

We're *inside* Homan Sphere. It's like a planet turned
inside out, with land where the sky should be. The view
makes my head swim, but I keep staring. I try to look
near the "sun" without looking *at* it, and when I squint
just right I see glinting lines of heavy cable suspending
what must be an open plasma reactor. Behind this tiny
faux star, the far side of the sphere hides in darkness.

"Incredible," I say under my breath. When I glance at
the Legionnaires, they aren't even bothering to look up. I
don't know if they've seen it too many times before, or if
being part of a human hive mind ruins you for appreciat-

ing extreme feats of engineering.

I look to the left hemisphere, not letting my eyes drift too far up this time, and see neatly delineated blocks. Most are shades of green flecked with shoots and spots of other color, but there are also shimmering fields of golden wheat and fallow stretches of dark soil. There are more gray compounds sown around the farmlands, and lengths of tube crisscross the whole of the Sphere.

Forests for air, farmlands for food—everything they need is generated right inside the prison. *Except water.* Maybe that's my exit strategy: wait for a water delivery and hijack the ship.

This huge rock has been hollowed, terraformed, and turned into a self-contained ecosystem: wholly artificial yet somehow natural too. I can't believe that MEPHISTO built a garden world for their fucking *prisoners*, while there are hundreds of colonized planets in the empire where people still can't go outside without protective gear.

I forget my awe for a second as a new realization creeps into my thoughts: How do I break Mookie out of a closed system? A prison inside a prison?

A loud hiss builds within the transit tube, then ends suddenly in a *shup* as a bullet-shaped pod slides to a halt within the pipe. Machinery shunts the pod out of the transit loop; the roof folds away and an android envoy emerges. It's unusually stocky, with extra armor plating on its torso and limbs. The head is lit up with a grainy image of a guard's face: young, male, and bored.

The envoy holds a waver across its chest, low enough that it doesn't block the lenses that act as its eyes. Weapons that tear apart flesh but leave inorganic material untouched are perfect for a prison where screws ride metal bodies via a holo-rigfrom behind the scenes via holo-rig.

The guard looks at me, then at the line of Legionnaires fanned out behind me. "All this for *her*?"

A Legionnaire to my right grunts. "Do not underestimate this prisoner. A recommended security routine was transmitted to Doctor Rathnam."

The lenses on the envoy's chest shift and swivel as the guard studies my face, then he raises his eyebrows and steps right inside my personal space.

"Yeah, we received it; Doctor Rathnam had this fabricated to specifications." He produces a large, segmented collar from behind the envoy's back and puts it around my neck. There's a series of quiet clicks as the collar tightens. "Normally we fit our prisoners with a bomb collar, but this is something else entirely." His voice is pitched high, with a strange lilt. It rises and falls steadily as he speaks, with no regard for what he's actually saying.

"For some reason, they want to keep your head where

it is, so there's no bomb in this one, but there are sensors that can detect abnormal brain activity. If you use the abilities Hamid warned us about, the collar will shock you. If you stray too far from your designated prison campus, it will shock you. If you try and remove the collar, it will shock you." He points over my shoulder and says, "If you try and enter that tunnel—"

"The collar will shock me?" I say.

He grins. "You catch on quick."

When the collar closed around my neck, the information scrolling across my HUD dried up as my aug-feeds were shut down. Now, all that's left is a blinking message: *DISABLED*. After a few seconds, even that is gone.

I lift my cuffed hands. "Are you going to take these off?"

"The restraints stay, but I'll take this," he says, then he grabs my cloak and lifts it off, snaking it down my arms and over the restraints.

The cloak was my second gift from Sera. The first was a bracelet that lets me slip through powershields; the same bracelet that's clamped beneath my handcuffs, hidden from sight. With the cloak gone, the guard quickly frisks me, cold android fingers prodding my flesh.

"I'll take it from here," he says. The envoy grabs me by the arm and yanks so hard I bash into the android's torso, then he spins and drags me toward the transit tube.

The Legion start moving and I turn to watch their formation shift and flow until they vanish into the darkness of the tunnel. The gate closes, and for all appearances it could be blocking a sewer drain or water runoff, not the prison's only dock.

I sigh and almost stumble as the guard hauls me along, my legs still aching. I'll be alone until I find Mookie, but loneliness was my life before; just me and Ocho, with a whole galaxy to hide in. So why do I *feel* so lonely now?

As we reach the car, we fall into the shade of one of the watchtowers. Hidden from the artificial sunlight, the shadows are black and cold as the void. I shiver and hope the screw didn't see, doesn't think I'm afraid.

We take a seat inside the transit pod and the roof closes as the vehicle slots into the transparent tunnel. The guard turns to look at me, his head twisting unnaturally while the android's chassis stays motionless. "Hold onto your hat."

We're launched forward and my neck snaps back, head thrown against the metal headrest. The guard laughs. Pinned by gravity, all I can do is look up and watch the surface of Homan Sphere shift above me.

• • •

The transit loop delivers us to a complex deep inside

Homan's forest. Fake sunlight falls dappled through the leaves; eyelids glow flesh pink when I close my eyes.

The compound is butterflied—two mirrored halves connected to a main hub—and the guard leads me to a central building with a sign reading *Maximum Security Site* over the entrance. The doors slide open as we approach and snap shut immediately behind us.

The main corridor smells of antiseptics with an underlying note of urine. A flash of childhood wracks my brain—girls waking up in screaming terror, sheets soaked with sweat and piss. In my memories it's the other girls who wake like that, pounding the ceiling with their manifesting telekinetic powers, but I was one of those girls too. Slapped by a caretaker and forced back into a soiled bed, feeling the wet patch turn cold while I cried, only knowing I'd slept because I woke later in the harsh light they used to simulate day.

I shake my head, as if that might clear the thoughts, but they linger.

Women dressed in green prison uniforms and metal collars move past, most of them walking slow or staggering. Some have had their scalps razored, others walk with heads low, faces hidden behind lank, dirty hair.

The guard takes me to a clinic. The lights inside are brighter than elsewhere, bleaching the skin of the patients lying in bed. Autodocs glide on wheeled feet, and a number of envoys line the far wall. These envoys are un-armored, torso panels white with caducei painted in red along the sternum, finely detailed wings spreading across the chest.

One of these medical envoys comes to life and walks toward me. A man's face is projected from the holo-unit at the neck: sharp nose, large eyes, and a white beard speckled with black.

He nods to my escort. "Good day, corporal."

"Sir," he replies.

I roll my eyes at the farce: wherever they're controlling the envoys from, these two are probably within spitting distance, heads hidden inside holo-rigs, playing at prison staff through their android toys.

"This is our new arrival?" he asks.

"Yes, sir; Mariam Xi. She was captured on Miyuki by Commander Hamid's forces and claims to be the terrorist responsible for the destruction of Commander Briggs's fleet, the murder of Commander Briggs, and the deaths of the personnel under his command."

"Is that so." The doctor's holographic face doesn't shift, but the envoy's lenses whir as he focuses his gaze on me. Standing this close, it's easy to see how his eyes don't quite meet mine. "I was informed we were taking delivery of an extremely high-risk prisoner, but I must admit I wasn't expecting someone quite so . . . petite."

"Death comes in all shapes and sizes," I say with a smirk.

He frowns, drawing deep lines across his face. "Deliver the prisoner's cloak to storage;" "I'll take her from here."

"Sir, the induction procedures—"

"I will handle it, *corporal*."

The doctor says the last word like a threat, but if the guard responds I don't hear it. His head flickers then disappears and the envoy leaves the room holding my bundled cloak, carried away by its own basic artificial intelligence.

"My name is Doctor Rathnam, and I'm responsible for all that happens inside Homan Sphere. As warden and senior physician, I have assigned myself as your caretaker."

It's like they deliberately chose the title "caretaker" to make my skin crawl.

"Mariam Xi," he says, as if to himself.

"People call me 'Mars.'"

"Come, walk with me." The envoy moves out into the hallway and I follow, walking beside the android as it ambles down the corridor.

"How do you feel, Mariam?"

I try to think of the best words to describe my particular mix of brain-fog and sluggish limbs. The best I can come up with is, "Drug-fucked."

Rathnam laughs, but it's a polite, insincere sound. "I'm certain the sedatives will be out of your system soon enough."

"Which is why you put me in this collar, right? I'm not sure a little zap is going to stop me, doc."

"I am well aware, Mariam: I have read the briefing documents which detail your abilities." We come to a hallway intersection and Rathnam stops. "I have decided we must take additional measures to ensure the safety of the other prisoners."

Rathnam's envoy raises its arm and motions to a guard escorting a prisoner toward the clinic. This prisoner is an older man, his back hunched and organic eyes cloudy with untreated cataracts.

"Your weapon, corporal?" Rathnam says, and the guard passes his waver over. Rathnam turns to face me and raises the weapon, pressing it to the elderly man's temple. "If you use your abilities to act out in any way, even in self-defense, one of your fellow prisoners will be killed. That might sound harsh, but you are a dangerous individual, and I take the well-being of my charges very seriously."

I'm sure you do.

His display complete, Rathnam returns the guard's sidearm. The old man sags, disappointment not relief, and we keep moving. A woman walks past and looks at me, her wide eyes windows to terror. She's wretchedly thin, and dark shadows line the hollows of her cheeks.

"You probably think this is the part of my speech where I say that we're going to break you—"

"I *was* waiting for that bit actually," I say.

"—but believe me when I say we hope to treat you well here. Commander Hamid has great plans for you, and it is my job to see them brought to fruition. One way or another, you will pledge your loyalty to her."

We enter the mess hall, empty but for a few prisoners mopping the floor and wiping down tables.

Rathnam continues. "I should also let you know that there are no space suits kept anywhere within Homan Sphere. So if you were to, say, break open the dock, you would be killing yourself and every other prisoner here."

"Not to mention the staff," I say, as a super subtle threat.

The doctor laughs, a loud blast that echoes off the high ceiling. "I am sorry to say that we are all safely ensconced on the surface of Seward, far away from your terrible abilities."

We come to a long corridor walled and roofed with glass. Outside the sun has set, and the leaves flutter in an artificial wind, but I can't hear their song.

The glass corridor leads us inside a multitiered building, four stories of cells rising above an open central corridor. Envoys patrol the walkways, some ridden, others empty-headed, all armed with wavers.

"And now we arrive at your new home, Mariam." Rathnam leads me to a large cell on the second floor. A powershield shimmers across the opening—beyond, lines of shield segregate the women into individual cells. They sleep on the ground, arms folded under their heads for pillows. A woman with two prosthetic arms has her cheek pressed flat against the polycrete floor. Another wears only collar and underwear; even through the blur of the shields I can see the lesions and cuts on her skin.

A segment of shield disappears and the doctor sweeps an arm toward the opening like it's a grand invitation. I step inside and hold my hands out to the envoy.

As he undoes the restraints, Rathnam says, "Escape is impossible. Remember that, and you will come to accept your new role more easily."

I nod and cover my bracelet with my other hand, hoping he doesn't notice it. It takes effort not to wince; beneath the bracelet my skin is broken, flesh bruised. "I understand," I say. It's true, but that doesn't mean I'm planning to comply.

CHAPTER NINE

I jolt awake as a shiver wracks my body; the cold touch of the polished cement floor has seeped into my bones.

I push up off the ground, my hands and arms oddly pale in the stark light falling from the single, illuminative panel that makes up the ceiling.

The powershields that separated us overnight have gone, but most of the women still lie in their spots, asleep or simply unwilling to move. The woman who's dressed in just her underwear sits in one corner, curled in a ball with legs pressed against her chest, head resting on her knees. Her limbs are bone-thin, and her black hair is streaked with white. She looks both juvenile and middle-aged, like living in this place has somehow aged her rapidly *and* rendered her childlike, dependent on author-ity figures for everything.

A larger woman sits on the cell's only toilet. She sees me looking and glares, then opens her legs and wipes herself, holding my gaze in an aggressive, animalistic display.

I shake my head and stand, then step over three prone

women as I walk to the shield wall enclosing the front of the cell. I turn back to face the woman on the toilet, give her a smile and a small wave, then step backward through the powershield. My whole body tingles, a surge of energy passing through me, igniting nerves in bizarre sensation.

The woman's face goes slack, her lips parting as her mouth hangs open. I spin away and start off at a jog.

Headless envoys man the sections of wall between cells, all on standby, the human guards likely working the daylight half of the Sphere. If the androids see me pass them, they aren't smart enough to realize I shouldn't be out of my cell this early.

I reach the stairs and bound down, footfalls gonging gently as I descend. A thin smile spreads across my face as I jog. It feels good to be moving, it feels *necessary*.

• • •

I shadow an envoy transferring from my wing to the core of the Maximum Security site. I stick close as it walks through the open steel door and slip through just before it clangs shut.

The central hub is beginning to stir, the hum of mechanical labor building with the approach of artificial dawn. I tail another envoy with my head low, acting like it's escorting me somewhere. When the envoy peels off into one of the clinic rooms, I switch to another. This one takes me through the reinforced door to what I guess is the men's wing.

Just like on the other side, it opens onto a corridor walled entirely in glass. Dull sunlight reflects off rich green leaves. If the prison wakes with Homan's sun, then I've got only minutes before the guards catch me.

The male prisoners are awake, and when I reach the cells a dull murmur of conversation ripples through the block. I approach the nearest lockup and push through the shield, startling an older man sat by the wall.

"Do you know Mookie?" I ask, voice quiet.

He narrows his eyes like he's trying to think, but he stays silent.

"Does anyone know Mookie?" I ask, louder this time.

The men all turn and look at me. One of the prisoners says, "How the fuck?" Another just mumbles, "Emperor's crack hair." If they know anything, they're too startled by finding me in their cell to say.

I duck out, and the men move as if caught in my orbit, drifting to the powershield to watch me slip into the next cell.

"Mookie?" I say. The men stare blankly, and I step back out.

At the far end of the block an envoy's head lights up as

the guards start their rounds.

"What the hell?" she says when she sees me. She starts running. The envoy's forearm opens, armor segments parting as a stun-baton emerges to jut perpendicular from its wrist.

"I know Mookie." A raspy voice speaks up.

I turn and see a wall of gaunt faces staring at me, unable to tell who spoke. "Where is he?" I ask, but no one answers.

The guard is almost on me now. I lift my arm and shove the envoy so hard it sails through the air. The collar around my neck reacts; skin burns and electricity sparks through my body. I collapse as the android crashes to the ground with a metallic clatter.

• • •

By the time the guards drag me back to the cell, I can almost walk under my own power. *Almost.*

The prisoners must be at breakfast now, because the other women's cell blocks are all empty. Not mine—it's packed with as many screws as prisoners, the women lined up against the back wall, the guards facing opposite.

Doctor Rathnam stands between the two groups, riding a guard envoy now, but somehow looking *less* authoritative in the armored android than in a medical one.

"Sergeant Ramirez!" Rathnam barks. "How did this happen?"

A guard steps forward, an older woman with as many facial tattoos as wrinkles showing in her holo-projection. She scans me up and down, then settles on my wrist.

"Sir," she says, "this device allowed the prisoner to escape. It should have been found and removed at induction."

I smirk at Rathnam.

The sergeant takes the bracelet off and snaps it in half. Losing one of my few reminders of Sera hurts more than I thought it would.

Rathnam pulls the envoy's waver sidearm from its holster and points it at the line of prisoners. "What did you think would happen, Mariam?" he says, sounding disappointed. He doesn't wait for an answer; he pulls the trigger and there's a sound like a robotic critter squeaking, following by a wet *pock*.

I don't even know the woman's name, but she's dead and toppling forward impossibly slow. She has brown hair, green eyes, and a gaping head wound.

"I told you what would happen if you used your powers."

I grab Rathnam's envoy and crush it, those useless plates of armor buckling as its internal machinery sparks and dies. The shock is less brutal this time, but still I scream as electricity lights up my insides. I fall to the ground panting, brought down to the level of Rathnam's envoy and his victim.

The larger woman drops to her knees beside the corpse, face twisted in anguish.

"You should not continue to test me," Rathnam bellows from a different android. This one points its weapon at the kneeling woman, but Ramirez steps forward.

"You don't need to kill Kirino too, sir; I think Xi has learned her lesson."

I look up and struggle to focus on the guard. Her holo-projection has close-cropped hair, which reminds me of Trix, which makes me think of Mookie. *Remember: you came here to save him, not to kill these women.*

I breathe in deep, trying to force my anger down, to imagine it seeping out through the soles of my feet.

"I expected better from a sergeant, Ramirez," Rathnam says, holstering his weapon.

"But sir, I didn't—"

"Stockton," Rathnam says, ignoring the woman, "you are now promoted to sergeant. *Corporal* Ramirez, you will be reassigned."

Rathnam's face disappears, and the newly promoted sergeant walks along the row of inmates, his face stony, eyes glinting with excitement. "Your new cellmate,

Mariam Xi, is a mass murderer and a terrorist; Cortez here is only her latest victim," he says, motioning to the dead woman on the ground, her wound cauterized black around the edges but steadily leaking gore. "Either Xi behaves, or she will kill you all. You should *encourage* her to behave." He lets that hang in the air a moment. "Dismissed."

The guards about-face and leave, and after a few moments the women move away from the wall, giving Kirino and the corpse of Cortez a wide berth as they filter slowly through the cell opening.

A hand touches my arm; the woman in her underwear, crouching beside me with one arm across her chest.

"We're late for breakfast," she says, helping me up from the ground.

"Sorry," I say; "that's my fault too."

Even this close, I can't guess at her age. The skin of her face is discolored and slack, but there's something in her eyes—something like hope or kindness. I feel the sudden urge to give her my shirt, or my pants, but something tells me that would only make her more of a target.

We start down the hall, and she asks in a quiet voice, "Where did you go?"

"To the men's wing, to look for a friend of mine."

"I'm Ali," she says, like the mention of a friend reminded her she should introduce herself.

"Mars," I say.

"Is it true that you killed a lot of people?"

"I killed a lot of MEPHISTO, not sure that counts." I grin and turn to look at Ali, and she smiles. I lean in closer. "What are you in for?"

She's silent for a second. "I come from Easa. I was arrested when MEPHISTO was sent in to quell the situation there."

"You were part of the revolt?" I ask.

She shakes her head minutely. "Protests, petitions, that sort of thing."

"That's all?"

"It was enough for them to bring me here."

I've seen footage from Easa: the protests labelled as riots, the crackdown, the trials. I can imagine Ali, back before this place turned her hair white, projecting holo-banners on skyscrapers, hacking city loudspeakers to blast protest messages, thinking her citizenship meant she could safely criticize the empire.

"I was expecting anarchists and terrorists here, not protesters."

"They called me a 'dangerous agitator,'" she says in her mouse-small voice, and we both laugh.

"Easa was years ago; have you been here all this time?"

Ali nods.

"If you know some people here, maybe you could help

me find my friend? Get the word out that I'm looking for him?"

Ali looks at me, eyes tight, like she's trying to decide if she should get involved or not. After a moment she says, "Okay."

When we reach the cafeteria, every head turns to face me. Word must have already spread about the way I crushed Rathnam's envoy, about how I "killed" Cortez.

I've spent my whole life as a pariah, but never so publicly. It's almost funny.

Take a good look, ladies, because I won't be here for long.

CHAPTER TEN

It doesn't take long for a routine to form.

I'm woken each morning by an absence of sound when the interior powershields go down. Though the steady drone stops, the cell's ceiling glows endlessly. There's always a rush for the toilet, and I try not to listen as my bladder sits hot in my abdomen with a dull ache.

I can't sleep without the buzzing hum, but I barely sleep with it. I lie on one side until that hip begins to hurt, then move to the other. All through the night collars clank against the floor as women shift in their sleep. Some of them strip and bundle their clothes up like a pillow. I try it once, but the floor is too cold.

Sometimes, in the middle of the night, I think I feel Ocho curled up against my belly. My fingers reach to touch her but find only void. I miss that tiny jerk.

. . .

I wake earlier than usual, blink, then close my eyes and watch the black-pink churn of flesh inside my eyelids.

The shields hum, overlapping sounds building a wall of white noise. I'm seconds away from falling back asleep, then silence drops like a stone into water.

I keep my eyes shut and listen to the women stir, then I hear a voice hissing in a coarse whisper. "You killed my girl."

I raise my head and see Kirino kneeling, staring at me as she works her jaw.

I sit up. "*They* killed her."

"Because of you."

I shake my head, but don't bother to argue. "I'm sorry," I say, and shrug because I know the apology isn't enough.

Kirino grunts as she stands. "How about I kill your girl?" she says, walking over to Ali. She rests her hand on the top of Ali's head, fingers slipping between the folds of her hair.

"She's not 'my' anything."

Kirino grabs a handful of hair and I push up off the floor fast, then sway for a second as the blood rushes to my head.

"Why don't you just fuck off, Kirino?"

Every pair of eyes in the cell is on me except Ali's, which are stuck fast to the ground.

"*What* did you say?" Kirino takes a step forward, making a show of shoving Ali's head away as she releases it. Her eyes are the darkest brown, almost black even under the bright lights of the cell. Her head is shaved, but if it was only done in prison, it suits her.

"I said 'fuck off.' This place is bad enough without you acting like an alpha bitch."

Kirino stares at me, face twisted in a snarl. "Are you trying to get someone else killed?"

"I don't need my powers to kick your ass," I say, though I can't remember the last time I fought without them.

A few long seconds pass, and the women sitting between us scurry out of the way. Just when I think she might back down, Kirino charges across the gap. She slams into me and I start elbowing the back of her head as we fall. We hit the polycrete hard. Kirino pushes herself up and punches me in the mouth. She pulls back to hit me again, but I slide my head out of the way just in time to hear the flat smack of her knuckles hitting the ground. She makes a wounded sound and freezes long enough for me to strike her in the jaw. Her teeth clack as they snap shut, and there's a burst of pain in my wrist. She replies with another punch that smacks my head into the floor.

She hits me again and again. I cover my head with my arms and wait for the next hit, but instead a voice yells, "Stand down, prisoner."

A segment of the powershield dissipates as two screws enter the cell. Kirino holds her hands up as one of them yanks her off me.

"You wanted to see the alpha, bitch," she says, then she winks.

One of the envoys pushes her aside while the other lifts me to my feet. "Mariam Xi, you are required to attend an interview."

I don't say anything, I just glare at Kirino as they lead me away.

• • •

We reach the glass-walled corridor linking the women's wing to the central hub. As we approach, the door at the far end opens. That familiar smell of antiseptic wafts in, washing the scent of tightly packed women from my nose.

The guard leads me past the clinic where I met Doctor Rathnam, past empty surgical theatres, each stocked with a chrome-plated autosurgeon glistening under ceiling lights. We come to a large, reinforced door with an access panel on one side. The guard leans across me to reach the panel, blocking my view while she keys in a code.

She stands back and I study the woman's face glowing in the holo-unit. She has a large hooked nose, and hair in a black ponytail long enough that it ends abruptly at the edge of the holo-field. The envoy's stance is too rigid, even for military personnel, but I don't know if that's *her* posture coming through, or just the robot's.

The doors beep and open. A mix of organic scents greets me: earthy tones of shit and sweat, the sharp metallic hints of blood. Behind this there's a chemical smell—sweet but dirty, like the sweat-stink of your bed-sheets after you sleep off a metamethamphetamine binge.

The guard takes me by the arm. "Come along, pris-oner."

At first I walk right along with her, not wanting to give her an excuse to yank hard on my arm like every other bastard guard, but when I see the other prisoners I begin to slow.

We're in a large expanse, wide open except for the powershields that define three group cells. The men are on the side of the room closest to their wing, with the women opposite. A third cell in the center houses the people that don't fit either of those narrow gender modes.

The male cell is filthy—floor and wall smeared with feces—and more densely populated than the other two. Most of the men look starved or beaten, or both. A few are missing limbs, and as I remember the surgical rooms I feel a chill drift along my spine.

We move past the group cells to smaller, solitary ones. They have solid doors with inset windows, and as we pass I get a glimpse of a dozen wretched prisoners. Each one is naked; some are barely visible in silent, pitch-black rooms, others are lit up bright, their cell doors vibrating with relentless sound. All are kept standing, strapped to hooks emerging from ceiling or wall.

There's a guard inside one of the cells, blood coating the android's metal fists. The prisoner's face is bruised and bleeding, his mouth a hollow maw devoid of teeth. Before I realize, I've stopped walking. The guard isn't even questioning him, he just rains blow after blow onto the man's torso as the prisoner hangs silent. Blood pools at his feet, vivid red against the white cell floor.

"Xi," the guard escorting me says, firmly, yanking me forward.

I keep walking. The only thing that stops me from interfering is the knowledge that they'd kill the poor bastard if I did.

Maybe I should have killed him. Would that have been murder or mercy?

•••

Beyond the torture cells there's a small corridor lined with doors. When we reach the door marked *203*, the guard lets go of my arm to unlock it. I step inside before she has reason to grab me again and come face-to-face with myself: hair limp and dirty, face slack.

The room is brightly lit, all four walls paneled in either mirror or one-way glass. In the center is a small metal table and two chairs. Doctor Rathnam's envoy sits in one of the chairs, his face pointed down like he's reading off a shard, though his envoy's hands are empty.

He motions to the other chair. "Please, take a seat."

I do as he says, and the guard closes the door behind her then moves to the corner behind the doc. The surface of the table is scratched and scuffed; it resounds when I tap a beat with my fingernails.

After a minute, Rathnam coughs. His envoy hand moves to cover his mouth a response to his movements inside the holo-rig. He clears his throat. "Let's begin, shall we?"

He seems to be waiting for a response, but I just keep tapping, listening to the dull *ting*.

"I want you to tell me what brought you here," he says, tone friendly.

"A ship," I say, deadpan. "I couldn't tell you what type it was."

He offers a polite smile. "How many people have you killed since you arrived, Mariam?"

"*I* haven't killed anyone."

"You knew the consequences of using your powers," he says, his pitch rising slightly, like he's rebuking a small child. "But perhaps you don't really care about these strangers . . ."

The wall behind the doctor turns transparent and for a split second my heart sinks as I think they found out about Mookie. It's not him though; on the other side of the glass a guard aims a waver pistol at a prisoner with four prosthetic limbs. His eyes drift over me before snapping back, and that's when I remember him too: the bodychopper from Aylett Station with the deliberately disproportioned limbs.

The bodychopper nods. I look back to Rathnam.

"Do you know this man?" he asks.

"No," I say. It's not really a lie, because I don't know the guy's name. As far as I know, his name is Chopper.

Half the wall changes into a large viewscreen showing two packs of people facing off down a wide corridor.

"We have security footage that proves otherwise." As Rathnam speaks, the recording rolls, volume muted. It shows me using my abilities to wreak a little havoc before Miguel drags me out of the fray, and it shows Chopper, all his friends, and all the bizarrely altered genehackers, fighting MEPHISTO troops.

Watching the reverse of the footage, Chopper smiles; on video he dismembers one soldier and punches another so hard they're lifted off the ground.

"After that fight," Rathnam says, "you continued your

rampage elsewhere on Aylett Station."

The video cuts to the gaudily colored carpet of a casino, though I've never been to any of the ones on Aylett. Which is why I'm confused when I see myself walking down an aisle of poker consoles. I tear the machines from the floor and throw them aside, crushing innocents and Station Security alike.

Chopper squints, first in confusion, then disgust.

"This is bullshit," I say. "I never went to a casino, I never killed any honeymooners. I went to the—" I cut myself off. I went to the docks, where there aren't any cameras, and I rescued Mookie, Squid, and Trix. But I can't tell Rathnam that. I can't give him the ammunition. "It's not true, Chopper," I say, holding the man's gaze until he looks away.

"You seem to believe you're fighting a righteous war against MEPHISTO, but look at this." Rathnam lifts a hand, motions to the screen. "You're a remorseless killer; no more, no less."

Killer? You don't know the half of it.

"I ask again," Rathnam says as the footage flickers out of view, "*why* are you here?"

I shift my weight and it feels like my ass bones are grinding into the hard seat. "I haven't heard the actual charges, but I assume it's for something like 'Crimes against MEPHISTO.'"

"Then you admit to killing twenty-three thousand, seven hundred and twelve MEPHISTO personnel?" he asks, raising an eyebrow.

I tap my fingers until Rathnam continues.

"I'm not trying to trick a confession out of you, Mariam; I'm merely trying to ascertain your mental state, to find out if you're aware of all the harm you've caused."

"That's the official tally, then: twenty-three thousand and something?" I ask, staring down at my twitching fingers.

"Twenty-three thousand, seven hundred and twelve."

I nod. "I couldn't have told you the figure, but it sounds about right."

"Do you regret murdering all those people?"

With my head lowered I can see the symbol for Xi tattooed on the back of my hand, the ink patchy and the lines blown out after all these years. A doctor just like Rathnam gave it to me when I was a child, except that doctor was with me in the flesh, because they weren't afraid of us when we were little. I remember it all—the black latex gloves pinning my wrist and fingers so I couldn't squirm while the tattoo machine moved across my skin, mechanism humming, needle a blur. I remember the ink and plasma leaking from the wound, I remember screaming that I was sorry, trying to figure out what I'd done wrong, why they were punishing me. But most of all I remember the awful fucking pain that no child should have to go through.

"No," I tell Doctor Rathnam, "I don't regret it at all."

"That is a shame, Mariam. Those people you killed had families, they had dreams and desires."

"When I was a little girl, I dreamed of walking on grass. I wished to go one day without getting stuck with a fucking needle."

"You mean to say the treatment you experienced as a child justifies mass murder?"

"What I mean to say is, Briggs didn't have to chase me.

"Imagine you build a fire, but you realize it's burning way hotter than you planned; do you run into it, or do you step back and give it space?"

One side of the doctor's mouth curls up. "Your analogy doesn't quite serve your purpose, Mariam. You would do whatever you must to bring the raging fire under control, before it burns down your whole house."

"Doc, some houses are meant to burn."

CHAPTER ELEVEN

Twenty-three thousand, seven hundred and twelve. Twenty-three thousand, seven hundred and twelve.

The mantra of guilt runs through my head as the guard takes me back to the cell. The interrogation took hours to get precisely nowhere, but at least they left Chopper alone.

As I pass through the mess hall, none of the gathered women look up from their plates. Seeing that inedible mush, I don't feel hungry, even if I did skip breakfast for Rathnam's "interview." The smell of overcooked vegetables hangs thick in the air: dank and lifeless.

Twenty-three thousand, seven hundred and twelve.

Fuck Rathnam—trying to use remorse against me. No one ever apologized for what they did to me, Sera, and the other children. How many have died for their projects? How many have they killed to make their human weapons?

When the guard takes me back to the group cell, it's open and empty; the other women must be eating, or having their walk in the recreation area. I take advantage of the vacant room to pace. I scratch the back of my head and wince, feeling a bump where Kirino struck my head against the ground.

I feel crazed almost: angry and quickened. I want to flex my mind and feel something break, but all I can do is pace.

"Anxious?"

Ali's standing just inside the cell holding a small bundle.

"More like agitated," I say. "Maybe bored."

She frowns, then asks, "Have you eaten?"

I'm about to tell her what I think of the prison's food when she peels back the wrapping on her parcel, revealing two roasted legs of whatever poultry they use for meat in this place.

"How did you get that?"

"I know someone in the kitchen. Here," she says, offering me one.

I take it and at first I'm disappointed that it's cold, but then I bring it close to my face and the scent of it fills my nose: no spices, no sauce, just the rich, fatty smell of dark meat. The skin cracks as I bite through it and the crispy outer layer gives way to soft flesh. I groan as I tear the meat away, then smile at Ali as I chew.

We sit against the rear wall of the cell, silent as we eat. I strip all the meat and start chewing on the cartilage at the joint for any residual flavor. I break the bone in half and suck at the marrow, but stop in disgust—cold, it's just flat tasting and gritty.

"Thanks," I say.

Ali bumps her shoulder against mine. "I thought you'd be hungry after the session."

"Nothing like a long, drawn-out interrogation to work up an appetite," I say it lightly, but when I glance at Ali her face has gone slack. "You've had your share of interviews too?"

Ali nods. "I must've given up everyone I ever knew, but it doesn't end."

"Is everyone in here political?" I ask.

"Everyone I've spoken to."

"Even Kirino?"

Ali nods. "She led the miner's revolt in the Mohsin Belt."

I make a noise like I understand, but I'm not familiar. "Has she always been so aggressive?"

"I don't know what she was like before, but they say she lost her wife during the revolt."

"That could change a person."

"She's always had someone in here, though," Ali says. "You always say yes to her; it's not worth it to fight."

"That's fucked," I say, and Ali nods.

After a few silent moments, Ali changes the subject: "Did that hurt?" She points to the tattoo of three lines on the back of my hand.

"Yes," I say.

"What does it mean?"

"It's the letter Xi in the Greek alphabet."

"That's cool," Ali says. "Why did you get it?"

I exhale sharply through my nose. "Because when MEPHISTO experimented on me as a child, they needed some way to group us together."

"Oh," Ali says.

I run my thumb over the jagged edge of the snapped bone, then put it in the waistband of my pants.

Eventually Ali asks, "Those experiments: that's why they're so scared of you?"

I nod.

"What can you do?"

"I could tear this whole place apart."

• • •

I jolt up. I must have been asleep, but I'm wide-awake now; heart thumping, adrenaline lighting up my veins.

Twenty-three thousand, seven hundred and twelve.

Muscles ache from the cold, hard floor, but my mind buzzes and sings. The other women are asleep still, all except Kirino. She's sitting cross-legged, and when she sees me looking at her she winks.

Her features were probably attractive once, before she spent years in the asteroid mines, before she got locked away at Homan. It's hard to know for sure when she's always either leering or sneering.

I lie back down and push Kirino from my mind.

• • •

I wake late the second time, and already the other women are lining up to exit the cell. I join the line and Kirino edges up behind me. I put my hand over the jagged bone in the waistband of my pants and wait, but she doesn't touch me.

She sticks close as we walk through the shield opening and out into the corridor, a large presence I can sense just over my shoulder. She leans close and says quietly, "What kind of a name is 'Mookie' anyway?"

I stop dead in my tracks, and she jostles me hard as she walks past.

"What did you say?"

Kirino laughs and keeps walking.

She reaches the mess hall and I rush to catch up. I grab her by the shoulder and spin her around. "What the fuck did you just say?" I repeat through gritted teeth.

A guard standing in the corner bellows, "Xi, calm yourself," but they don't move.

Kirino takes a small step to bump into me. I move back and sweep my eyes down her body, taking in the words "Homan Sphere" stenciled on her tunic above a serial number somewhat lower than twenty-three thousand, seven hundred and twelve.

She turns her head to motion to Ali. "Your girl was asking after him for you, but I found him first," she says. "I told the guards—they should have him by now."

"You fucking snitch."

She shoves me hard and I stumble backward, knocking into an older women with intricate white patterns tattooed over all her visible skin. Kirino is already moving at me; she hits me once in the jaw and I stagger and duck under the second punch. I step back, beyond her reach, tasting the blood that lines my teeth and gums.

"I'm going to enjoy this," she says.

I spit red on the floor. "Really? Rare for a person to enjoy their own death."

Her nostrils flare as she leaps forward and throws a fist. She hits me in the face and hot blood floods the back of my throat. I cough and spit, spraying blood on us both. I start panting, focusing on my breath so I don't lash out. There's a dull ache in my mind: the reservoir of unspent rage.

A crowd of women forms around us; their cheers a soundtrack accompanying every move as we dodge and dance. Kirino swings and I block my face with one arm, and with the other I reach into my waistband and grab the piece of bone.

She lands another punch and my nose jolts with pain. I feel it run with wet warmth, but with my mediag switched off, I can't know if it's broken.

I grip the bone like a dagger and thrust it into her neck. It digs into the skin and Kirino's face goes blank. She stumbles back as I pull the bone from the wound. Blood gushes down Kirino's neck, then between her fingers when she puts a hand to her throat.

"You void-damned bitch," she splutters, breathless.

I rush forward, jump at her, and ride her down to the ground as she falls. She tries to push me off, but I stab her again. I'm not doing this for Mookie, I'm not even doing this for me, I'm doing it because *fuck you*, because *fuck every piece of shit that uses their strength, their power, their privilege to harm those weaker than them*. I keep stabbing and it's the first time since getting here that I've felt alive, that I've felt whole.

The ragged gouges in Kirino's neck ooze blood with a slowing beat. The bone slips from my blood-slick hand, stays stuck in her skin.

I'm panting and my throat is raw; I hadn't even realized I was screaming. My heart is racing and blood drips from my nose and mouth to spatter on Kirino's static face. Last time I was soaked in sweat straddling a woman, the circumstances were *very* different.

If I'm honest, this is nearly better.

I look around, and all the women surrounding me stare in horror. I lift my head and try to slow my breath.

"Get off the inmate, Xi."

I stand and the circle of women parts, revealing a guard with their sidearm at Ali's head. In the rush of the fight I didn't process the other sounds I was hearing—the sharp yelp Ali made when they grabbed her, the clatter of her tray hitting the ground.

I didn't even use my abilities, but it's not about the rules. They have to try and control me, have to do their best to break me. My whole life they've tried to break me, because an unbroken witch is too powerful, too great a threat.

"Fuck this," I say, and use my mind to tear the collar from my neck, feeling one short spark as it reacts to my powers. I break it into a thousand tiny pieces that wash down my body as they drop to the floor. Next I take hold of the envoy threatening Ali and crush it, then I grab the rest of the screws lining the wall of the cafeteria and crumple them—android bodies bending in unnatural arrangements as their spines and limbs are mangled.

I feel like electric sex, like the woman who broke

Death's heart and face.

"Get out of here, Ali," I yell, "run, hide," but my voice sounds deadened by my bleeding nose, and a Klaxon has started blaring. I don't know how much of it she heard.

I flee the mess hall and run into a dozen envoys charging down the corridor, armed with stun-batons. I don't stop moving, I just blast them apart. There's a pop as their torsos explode, then the sharp patter of debris showering the walls, ceiling, and floor. I keep running, keep rampaging.

I leave the women's wing and tear through the sealed door that leads to the central building. I pass the clinics, and reach the group cells.

There are four people standing in the center of the room—Rathnam and Sergeant Stockton pointing their weapons at Chopper and another prisoner with dark skin and a shiny scalp, his shackled arms lined with fine bioluminescent tattoos that glint beneath the room's bright lights.

Mookie.

Everything else goes out of focus, and there is only Mookie standing ahead of me. He's naked, hands covering his junk. It's not the first time I've seen him nude, but it's shocking how much his body has changed. His skin is discolored, covered in bruises and lacerations. He was thin before, but now he looks like a skeleton with skin—each of his ribs clearly visible, expanding as he breathes, and there are deep hollows behind each of his collarbones.

When I finish examining his body and look up at his face, I see he's smiling—eyes bright, broad grin showing yellowed teeth. *He's fucking smiling.* I never thought I'd be so happy to see someone that wasn't Ocho.

The squeal of a waver brings me back to the scene. Rathnam lowers his sidearm and Chopper falls forward, prosthetic knees clanking as he hits the floor.

"No!" I yell, but it's too late.

"Mariam," Rathnam calls out. "Before you act, I must warn you that your friend's collar is primed. If you destroy either of these envoys, he *will* be killed."

A red light blinks on Mookie's collar. There's a gap beneath the segmented metal on either side of his neck, like they haven't bothered to adjust it since they starved him half to death.

I breathe in through my mouth, my nose completely blocked and probably broken. I try to say, "OK," but can't make the hard *K* sound. I raise my hands and put them behind my head.

I look at Mookie and give a tiny nod to let him know that everything is going to work out.

Everything is going to work out, isn't it? I came this far so it has to. It fucking has to.

CHAPTER TWELVE

They fabricate another collar. Once it's around my neck, four guards escort me to the clinic, which is pointless overkill now that I know Mookie's at risk. I guess *they* don't know he's the only reason I'm here.

A wide swathe of blood covers the front of my tunic, the wet fabric sticking to me like a second skin.

As we enter one of the examination rooms, the autodoc stationed inside comes to life. It takes a couple of goes to scan my retina past my swelling eye sockets. It shines a light from one of its fingertips into my left eye, then the right. It orders me to stand while it watches me with its lenses clicking quietly, before telling me to sit.

The autodoc's fingers are cold and hard as it pinches my nose. Its hand actuators whir for a short moment, then it snaps my nose back into place with a shock of pain and a burst of speckled white across my vision.

It sprays antiseptic on my wounds without bothering to warn me. The spray stings in my eyes only slightly less than in the splits across my lip and the bridge of my nose.

"Apply ice to minimize swelling," it says, synthesized

voice too bright for these circumstances.

Yeah, I'm sure the guards are prepping an ice pack for me right now.

"These painkillers and antibiotics will help with the healing process." The autodoc's arm folds backward at the elbow. Segments of the forearm's shell split apart, leaving an empty hollow wide enough for a person to fit their arm inside. I shift back from the autodoc, but a guard is there. She pushes me forward and keeps a hand on the back of my neck.

I sigh, and slide my left arm into the gap. The mechanism in the autodoc's upper arm ticks and whirs, then three needles emerge. Green light stripes across my arm and I turn my head just as the needles plunge into my skin. I chew the inside of my cheek to stop myself from making noise.

I pull my arm free and the autodoc turns away, apparently done. I stand and pitch to one side, then right myself. The guard shifts her hand from my neck to my arm, the android's metal fingers pressing into the fresh puncture wounds.

The painkillers kick in and the various stinging and aching parts of my face fade as the guard leads me from the clinic.

• • •

"Strip."

We're in a small tiled room with a drain in the floor, but no showerheads or taps on the wall. The envoy blocks the exit.

There's a *squick* as my bloodstained tunic comes away from my skin, and a wet slap when I drop it to the floor. I take off my bra next, then peel off my pants and underwear together.

The guard crosses the room and kicks the discarded clothes aside.

She walks back to the door and thumps one of the tiles. It swings open, revealing a coiled length of bright-blue hose. Before I can speak she sprays me in the face. The water is so cold it forces the air from my lungs and I pant and sputter as I struggle to breathe. I hang my head and hug myself as she runs the blast of water over my body. Looking down, I watch the whorls of diluted red swim toward the drain.

All I wanted to do was save Mookie; get inside Homan, find him, and leave. I wasn't planning to kill everyone who had a hand in running this place, but plans change . . .

"Turn around," she yells over the roar of the hose.

The water hits my back with enough force to push me toward the wall. Soon she turns off the water and I stand shivering while she replaces the hose.

"Alright, prisoner, come with me."

"Are you going to give me a towel?"

The woman grins.

"What about something to wear?" I ask.

"I knew I forgot something," she says, then she closes a pair of handcuffs around my wrists. "If you wanted clothes, you shouldn't have gotten blood all over your uniform."

• • •

She pulls me by the short chain between the cuffs, as though I'm an animal struggling against its leash. My feet slap wetly across the floor. Long after that sound has dried, water drips from my hair and rolls down my back.

We reach the cells of the central building and walk past the large group units to the small, solitary rooms. She pushes me into one of these bare cells—a two-meter cube, every surface the same white polyplastic, glowing diffusely.

I don't see the guard work any controls, but a slit opens in the ceiling and a chrome hook protrudes through the gap.

"I'm not doing this," I say; "get me Rathnam."

The guard ignores me, and after a few seconds the far wall of the cell comes to life with an image of Mookie's face. It's only when I see the light on his collar blinking that I realize it's a live feed. She doesn't remind me what will happen to Mookie if I misbehave, she doesn't make any threats, she just says, "Rathnam will see you when he's ready, and not a moment sooner."

"You can't do this," I say, but even I hear the lack of conviction in my voice.

She grabs my arms and lifts them until the chain of my cuffs is over the hook's curl. There's a ticking sound overhead as the hook retracts, pulling my arms and lifting me up until I can barely touch the floor with the tips of my toes.

The guard exits the cell, leaving only silence behind.

. . .

My heart beats hard, struggling to push blood up to my hands. I can't feel my fingers, can barely feel the cuffs digging into me, hard metal against bone.

The cell's walls, floor, and ceiling dim so slowly that at first I'm not sure it's happening. Soon I'm in darkness.

My breathing sounds ragged, too loud. It scrapes my ears. My pulse thrums against my collar. My head rocks with the pulse, forward and back on the tide of my blood.

"Let me out!" I yell, but the words dissipate on the walls, refuse even to echo back at me.

The pain in my shoulders switches from sharp to dull at intervals. I drop my head and hang from the hook, let the cuffs carve deeper into skin.

I close my eyes—black.

I open them—black; inky black that churns with impossible shades of dark. I see movement somewhere beneath me. I know the cube is two meters a side, but the moving shape is much farther away than that. It drifts and shifts as it approaches—soft, gray, with four white spots.

"Ocho?" I say, picturing those spots as her little paws.

I hear her *maow*, but she's not there. The darkness folds and swims. I close my eyes, but it's the same.

• • •

I jolt awake, screaming. The scream rattles my vocal chords, but I can't hear it. *The Emperor's Requiem* fills my head, skull vibrating with the deep tones of the dirge.

They've pulled the hook up higher now. Even stretched, my toes don't reach the floor, and I sway without purchase.

I shake against the hook in the roof and pain shoots up my arms as the blood returns to the muscles.

The walls of the cell begin to glow. The light builds, grows, consumes me; I look down, away from the walls, and watch my feet dissolve, bleached by light. I close my eyes against the bright; pinks and reds flash across my eyelids. I scrunch my eyes tight, but still the light burns through.

I yell for help, not knowing who I expect to come.

No one does.

The light holds me, refuses to let go.

The Emperor's Requiem ends and I hear sobbing. The sound falls away as I stop to take a breath. Just as I begin to yell, the song starts over.

. . .

It's dark again. Too dark. For a moment I think I'm dreaming; I think I'm dead.

I'm not, and I don't know how I feel about that.

My body shakes uncontrollably. The cold is so harsh my skin feels like it's burning.

There's a constant ticking, and I wonder which part of my body could make that sound. I've grown used to every noise this meat engine makes—the squirt of swallowing saliva, the bubbling groan of my empty stomach, the steady hiss of my lungs, the too-slow beat of my heart, the splash of piss on my feet. This noise is something else.

The floor rises beneath me, presses against the balls of my feet, then against my heels. For a second I think I'll be crushed, but then I realize: I'm being lowered.

I glance up but can't see the hook; I can't see anything. I shake my arms and hear the chain rattle. I pull and I yank and I start to cry, then I lift the chain from the hook and collapse.

I hit the ground and feel my heart stop. I hear one beat and then I wait, and I wait, feeling an empty-headed numbness falling—then it beats again. My head sputters and I rest it against the floor.

I curl up, trying to find solace from the cold. My arms are crossed over my chest, my knees are drawn close. I press my lips together to stop them shuddering. I bite down to stop my teeth from chattering.

I wait for sleep, or death.

CHAPTER THIRTEEN

The guard pushing me into the room of mirrors looks familiar: young, with sunken cheeks and dark eyes.

"Ah, Mariam, I'm so glad you're back." Doctor Rathnam stands beside the table in the center of the room. "Please, sit. You were about to tell me something important before Sergeant Stockton took you to the bathroom: what was it?"

I sit down and stare at Rathnam's medical envoy, trying to remember. The guard, Stockton, took me to the bathroom?

"I don't know what you're talking about," I say, voice a faraway whisper in my ears.

The guard came to me in that cube. He grabbed me by the hair, yanked me off the ground, and brought me here. There was no *before*.

"Come now, Mariam," Rathnam says. He takes a seat opposite me. "You remember. You were just about to give me information on the insurgency against the empire."

My brow furrows. After a second I start to chuckle, but it turns into a cough, pain rasping down my throat, ruined by the constant screaming in the box. "How often does that routine work?"

"Why don't we start with these two?" The mirror behind the doctor flickers, becomes an image of two faces.

I can't stop myself from gasping. Trix and Squid, staring straight ahead, faces blank. These aren't recent photos, they're a few years old at least. Squid in particular looks vastly different—their skin slightly darker back then, like they spent more time planet-side, soaking up sunlight.

"Patricia Clark," Rathnam says, "and the other who is known only as 'Squid.' These two were part of your cell. We know they assisted in your failed assault on Miyuki."

Failed, sure.

"There's no cell," I say, staring at their faces, wondering where in the void they might be. Are they nearby, like we planned, waiting for me and Mookie to escape? "They're my friends; that's all."

"Are you loyal to the emperor, Mariam?"

"What?" I say, confused, because it's not a question I've ever considered. I laugh, and either Rathnam passes a command to Stockton or the grunt takes some initiative: he crosses the room in two steps and backhands me. I tumble off the chair and hit the floor.

"Wrong answer," he says, standing over me.

After a few seconds Rathnam gets up and offers me his

envoy's hand, and lifts me from the ground.

I sit back down and Stockton stands his envoy in the corner behind the doc. He glares at me with his mouth twisted. I look away, but he's there at the edge of my vision, reflected endlessly in the opposing mirrors—an infinite series of assholes curving off toward an unseen event horizon.

"Are you loyal to the emperor?" Rathnam repeats.

"I don't care about the emperor," I say. "I don't care about politics, I don't care about the galaxy."

"We have evidence linking you to a group of insurgents responsible for attacks across imperial space."

"I don't go much for 'groups.'"

"Are you bisexual?" Rathnam asks.

My eyes roll of their own volition. I don't answer.

"Do you find yourself attracted to people regardless of their gender?" After a few moments, Rathnam pivots on his chair with a screech of metal on metal. He reaches into a bag and turns back to face me. It's tightly bundled, but I'd recognize that fabric anywhere. My hand reaches for the cloak before I can stop it.

"I was hoping to return this, but you need to demonstrate your cooperation before that can happen." He motions toward my naked body and says, "You would have something to cover yourself with."

I wasn't even thinking about that. I just want to hold

the cloak to my face and smell the scent I tell myself is Sera, but which is probably me, Ocho, and all her previous incarnations.

"I'm doing my best, doc, but I don't know what you're talking about. But if you give me the cloak anyway, maybe I'll go easy on you."

Rathnam laughs, three neat *has* that sound as mechanical as his android body. He asks, "Will the death of your two friends hinder the insurgency's efforts?"

"What?"

"Squid and Patricia." The hologram of Rathnam's head looks down, like he's reading something. "They were killed fleeing Miyuki."

"Bullshit," I say.

"The Legion intercepted them and ordered them to halt. When they refused, their ship was destroyed—a crusher of some sort, according to this report."

There's a stabbing pain in my chest, and my throat tightens thinking of Squid, Trix, and Pale. I shudder as I think of Ocho and Seven and all her old selves lost to the void, and I blink to stop the tears from forming. *It can't be true.* It fucking can't. I didn't come here to find Mookie just to lose Ocho and the others.

But he didn't mention Pale. If it were true, he'd know about Pale . . . wouldn't he?

"Are you sexually dominant or submissive?"

"What do you think?" I say, with a forced glibness.

"This isn't working," Stockton says.

Rathnam's head spins and he glares at the sergeant. His mouth moves, but I can't hear what he says. They talk back and forth, muted, then Rathnam nods.

The faces of Squid and Trix disappear as the wall turns transparent. My breath catches in my throat—not because Mookie's there beyond the glass, naked but for his bomb collar, but because he's strapped unconscious to an upright gurney accompanied by an autosurg. The robot works at Mookie's scalp with a disinfectant swab, painting his skin a greenish tint.

"Before you do anything rash, Mariam, you should know that your new collar has been modified: if it detects a spike of mental activity, it will trigger the detonation of Cadwell's collar."

"What are you going to do to him?"

"Nothing; if you cooperate."

I tear my eyes away from Mookie and look at the doctor. "And if I don't, you'll cut him to pieces?"

"He's too valuable for that. We make Legionnaires here, Mariam. Well, we begin the process. We install the necessary components to join them to the hive mind, but the body modifications are done elsewhere."

"I swear to Sera, if you touch him I will fucking kill you." I glare at the lenses in the chest of Rathnam's envoy and hope the man behind the machine is squirming, wherever he is.

Rathnam doesn't respond, his face holding its amicable mask. "Which member of your cell were you *involved* with?" he asks.

I think of Trix standing in the doorway while Mookie invites me into their bed.

"Is this man your lover?" When I don't respond, Rathnam says, "If you do not answer my questions, we will begin Cadwell's surgery."

"How did you find him?" I ask, stalling for time while I try to think of a plan.

"Kirino assured us we had to find your 'Mookie' to keep you under control. After we put word out among the prisoners, it didn't take long for someone to turn him in.

"Now: *is* he your lover?"

"No," I say. "He's not a member of any cell, and he's not my lover; he's a friend."

Rathnam stands and walks to the wall. He watches the autosurg for a moment, then says, "Restrain her."

Stockton's envoy clanks over behind me, and he puts his hands on my shoulders, forcing me down into my seat.

I shake my head. "What are you—don't—"

"Begin," Rathnam says.

"No!" I yell.

The autosurg rolls into position behind Mookie. Unlike the autodocs, surgery units aren't designed with bedside manner in mind, so there's nothing humanoid about them. They're simply compact wheeled platforms of lenses, sensors, and surgical equipment. The machine raises its finely articulated arm, and a scalpel emerges from its tip.

My mouth keeps moving, but no words form—all of my focus is on the scalpel, effortlessly slicing into the skin at Mookie's temple. The surgeon's limb circles Mookie and the blade rings his scalp.

I miss the vertical cut, but retch when the autosurg folds Mookie's scalp back, revealing white skull streaked with red.

"Who recruited you into the insurgency: Cadwell? Patricia? Squid?" Rathnam asks the question casually, keeping his tone conversational.

"No one recruited me," I say, voice frantic.

"Continue," Rathnam says.

Mookie's gurney shifts, lays him facedown at a forty-five-degree angle. I'm breathing hard now, my whole chest heaving as I struggle to stay calm, to avoid triggering my powers and Mookie's bomb collar.

A circular blade protrudes from the surgical hand-apparatus and I turn my head away, refusing to look as the saw squeals and whines, cutting into Mookie's skull.

"What do you know of the insurgency's plans? What are their next targets?"

"There is no insurgency," I say, struggling to get the words out between sobs.

Doctor Rathnam frowns. "Remember Cadwell, Mariam, and cooperate."

"I'm trying." I glance up and see the pink of Mookie's exposed brain and I screw my eyes shut tight.

"This is your final chance, Mariam. After the next step, there will be no going back."

"No," I plead. "Don't do it."

"I assume you know something of the physiology of the Legionnaires after your senseless killings on Miyuki," Rathnam says, intently watching the surgery beyond the glass. "You have experience with their reinforced skeleton and genetically toughened epidermis—but the metal skull is much more than armor plating."

"Shut up shut up shut up."

"The command and control interface is built into the skull plates. Nanowidth tendrils extend from the skull into the brain, overriding the individual will—each criminal becomes just one minuscule piece of individuality lost in a sea of the Legion."

I open my eyes and see the surgeon holding two pieces

of metal skull. "You can't do this."

"He will still be Cadwell, but he will also be the thousands of other people he's networked with. It's incredible, Mariam: humanity's first distributed consciousness!"

"And you use it as a fucking army. How imaginative."

If Rathnam heard me, he ignores it. "Where did the insurgency train you? Where is their base? How large is their army?"

I'm panting now, writhing in my seat, using every piece of strength left inside me to hold my powers in check, to keep the witch in her cage.

"I don't—" is all I manage to say before Rathnam orders the surgeon to carry on.

I scream and thrash. Tears run down my cheeks and my breath stops. My mouth moves and sounds form, but they aren't real words, they spill up from my horrified trance—mindless ramblings while my thoughts are blank. My mind is an endless void: black, empty. My body is a distant thing, cold and naked, shocked and screaming.

Disconnected, I recede on the tide of myself and leave Mookie to drown.

CHAPTER FOURTEEN

I sit in the rec area, looking up at the trees beyond the compound walls, feeling the scratch of the coarse, blueish grass through the fabric of my cloak. I've got nothing on beneath it—Rathnam just dropped the cloak on the table when he was done. I don't remember what questions he asked, but I remember my thoughts racing as I tried and failed to stitch together lies convincing enough to stop the surgery.

Rathnam ran out of questions long before the auto-surgeon finished, but he made me sit in that room while Mookie's entire skull was taken apart and replaced with metal. The autosurg installed glossy chrome implants into Mookie's ocular cavities, then put his skin back in place, knitting the folds together with geneprinted epidermis in geometric patterns.

A few women wander the yard. Most are alone, but some walk in pairs. I thought prisons were meant to be filled with gangs, formed like diamonds under the pressure of surviving, but I haven't seen anything like that in Homan. Maybe there are gangs in the farmlands—here in Max we're all too broken. Who has the energy to fight other prisoners when it's a struggle to hold onto yourself?

Kirino. My stomach quavers, and I want to be sick, but there's nothing in my stomach: I left it all on the floor of the interrogation room. Is this what remorse feels like? Guilt? It's different when you kill with your hands. I don't know why, but it is.

I didn't have to kill her; I did it because it was easier than dealing with her any other way. *She had it coming, though.* Did she have it coming? Or do I kill because it's easy?

I see a woman approaching, her hands straight at her sides, keeping the hem of her shirt low as she walks. I put a hand up to shield my eyes and accidentally bump my nose, still tender from where the autodoc fixed it. With the sun out of my eyes I can see it's Ali. They've given her a tunic, but still no pants.

"Hey, Mars."

"Hey."

"That's a nice cloak," Ali says. "The color really suits you."

I laugh nervously, still waiting for the churning in my stomach to calm. "Thanks." I rub a hand on my belly to feel the soft fabric against my skin. "When will they give you pants?" I ask.

"I don't know," she says as she sits beside me, "but this is better than nothing." She leans her head on my shoulder and looks up at the trees with me. "Kirino was worse than the guards," she says. "I'm sure there are women in here who'd thank you."

I'm thrown for a second, thinking Ali read my mind, but then I remember that the last time she saw me was during the fight.

I shake my head. "It's not a good thing I did."

Ali's head moves against my shoulder as she nods. "Yes, it was."

Two women walk past speaking some dialect of Spanish I'm not familiar with. I only catch a few words, but it's enough to know they're also talking about me killing Kirino.

"Are you doing okay?" she asks.

"I don't even know," I say.

"What happened?"

"I saw my friend."

"That's good," Ali says, brightly.

"They made him into one of them—they made me watch the surgery."

Ali doesn't say anything, but from her silence I guess she's lost friends to the Legion too.

A cold breeze pushes through the trees and we both shiver in unison, half-naked in different ways.

Eventually, after the leaves have fallen quiet again, Ali asks, "Could you really break everyone out of here?"

That wasn't what I was talking about when I said I could tear this place apart, but seeing her eyes—clear and wide with hope—I can't say no. "I could," I say. I break off a long blade of grass and run it between my thumb and forefinger, feeling its tiny fibers catch against my skin.

Ali sighs—I don't hear it, but I feel the way her body moves. Faux sunlight falls through shaking leaves overhead. It's serene, almost beautiful if I forget where we are. "Don't you get lonely sometimes?" she asks.

"I'm used to being alone," I say, though I can't stop Ocho looming in my thoughts, followed by Mookie, Squid, and Trix.

Ali nuzzles into me, as if to emphasize the subtext of her question. I put my arm around her, and I feel her head shift off my shoulder. In the corner of my eye I see her looking at me, but I don't face her.

I can sit here under a tree holding her, watching the accelerated approach of dusk, but that's all. Whatever else she might want, I can't give it to her. Not when I'm only here because someone else got too close, got caught up in my mess of a life.

She lays her head back down and sighs. If it's contentment or resignation, I can't tell.

. . .

Stockton comes for me before I've finished eating breakfast.

"Where is he?" I snap, but Stockton ignores me, grabs my arm, and lifts me from the seat.

Stockton marches me back to the central hub, room 203. He opens the door and shoves me inside.

Rathnam stands on one side of the room, accompanied by another envoy, headless, waiting for its rider. "Good morning, Mariam," he says, not sounding quite as bright as usual. "Please take a seat."

"Where's Mookie?"

Rathnam turns to face the blank envoy, then says, "Excuse me." His face blinks out.

I grunt in frustration, but put Rathnam from my mind. I stare at the woman in the mirror: the bags under her eyes are heavy and dark, while the rest of her skin looks paler than it should. Even at this distance I can see how greasy her hair is: shiny and lank. It's long, but not uniformly. There are scars on her head from where they cut open her skull to do things to her brain. Mostly she looks small, even weak. I harden my features and she does the same, and that's when I see the weapon MEPHISTO started making all those years ago.

Rathnam's face returns and he takes up Stockton's

usual position in the corner.

"Who are we waiting for?"

"We must be patient a little longer, I'm afraid," he says. "While we wait, perhaps we can continue our interview."

"Where's Mookie?" I ask again.

"Don't worry, Mariam. Your friend Cadwell is right here." Rathnam points at the mirror and I look back at my reflection. The image darkens by degrees until it disappears, replaced by Stockton's envoy and Mookie standing behind the glass. They've given Mookie clothes, but his face and head are badly swollen, and slits of silver peek out from bruised eye sockets.

I nod, but Mookie stays perfectly still. I worry that he's already interfaced with the Legion, but then he nods back, wincing at the movement.

"You could just call him 'Mookie'; everyone else does."

"And I could call you 'Mars,'" Rathnam says, "but I don't." He begins reading from Mookie's record: "Cadwell Amos Moreland—joined the imperial army at age seventeen, served in the 83rd Infantry Division as a combat medic. After five years of service, and thirteen tours, Moreland deserted his post while stationed on Scaraf. After a four-year gap he was apprehended by Commander Briggs. He has been languishing here for months now, abandoned by his friends; but he need never be alone again. Soon he will be Legion."

"We never abandoned him. We never abandoned you, Mookie."

Rathnam smiles. "You think I'm a fool, don't you? I knew from the start that you could not have been captured so easily unless you allowed it. I know you came here to free Moreland, but now it's too late."

I lean back in my seat. "I'm going to get him out of here, and then I'm going to kill you."

"Don't threaten me, *Mariam*," he says, finally dropping the veneer of politeness he's maintained all this time. "If only you had talked, you might have gotten your friend back, but you refused to betray the insurgency."

"We've been through this, *doc*," I say, matching the venom of his voice with a little of my own. "I don't know about any insurgency; if I did, I would have told you everything to stop you doing that to Mookie."

"What about the riot you started on Aylett Station? Your show of force against the military has inspired other such actions throughout imperial space. Not only that, but you were clearly cooperating with Aylett locals."

"I started that riot because I refused to let Briggs capture me, and the Ring One freaks joined in because they love any excuse to show off their mods. You see politics where the rest of us see survival."

"*Everything* is politics."

I roll my eyes and the doctor sneers. Standing behind

the glass, Stockton just looks bored. Remembering his slap, I guess he'd rather be inflicting violence than hearing about it.

"Cadwell will leave here soon to join his siblings in the Legion; the only question remaining is whether you leave with him, or whether I throw you into a box and forget about you."

"Leave with him?" I say, cautiously.

The other droid comes to life, holo-unit showing a woman's face—strong nose, sharp jaw and cheekbones, dark eyes, and rich brown hair curled to stay off her face. I don't normally pay much attention to hairstyles, but after weeks surrounded by unkempt prisoners and military-neat guards, her hair is sublime.

The woman doesn't speak; she just rotates the torso of her android slowly as the eye lenses take in the cell and the two figures behind the glass.

"I see you've already performed the operation, doctor."

"Yes; it was a complete success," Rathnam says, sounding pleased with himself.

The woman grunts. "Both of you leave; I'd like to talk to Mariam and her friend alone."

Stockton's envoy goes blank first, but its hand stays wrapped around Mookie's upper arm. Rathnam opens his mouth then closes it. After a few seconds, his face disappears too.

The woman paces across the room, momentarily obscuring Mookie from my sight with each lap.

She waves a hand in Mookie's direction. "You've seen what we do here, then, with the prisoners we find suitable?"

I nod.

"And you've experienced Commander Briggs's program firsthand; what a unique position to be in.

"Briggs was given children for his experiments, but we had to look elsewhere. A lot of prisoners died before we perfected the surgeries."

I recognize the pattern of her speech, if not the voice—it's the woman I spoke with before I arrived here; the leader of the Legion.

"We've met before, haven't we?" I say.

"Yes, briefly. Commander Zoe Hamid," she says, taking a seat opposite.

I cross my arms over my chest. "Things didn't go well for the last MEPHISTO commander who came looking for me."

She nods. "That's precisely why I'm here. We didn't take Briggs's program seriously before. Over a decade of training to produce psychics of varying ability and questionable loyalty? It seemed preposterous, until we saw what you did to him, how you single-handedly tore his fleet apart.

"I was serious before, Mariam; I want you to work for me."

I look past Hamid to Mookie and raise my eyebrows. I'm sure if his face weren't so badly bruised he'd do the same.

She laughs. "You might consider yourself an enemy to MEPHISTO, but I see your value. You've already been an asset: after you killed Commander Briggs, imperial intelligence uncovered his conspiracy. He had positioned a number of his subjects close to positions of power and influence. We don't know what his end goal was, but we can guess."

"Sera was right," I say, softly.

Hamid tilts her head, but continues. "Some of those women agreed to work with me."

"And the rest?"

"I did what I could for them, Mariam, but in the end they were executed."

"So now you've come here to make me the same offer? Be your pet voidwitch or die?"

"I'm giving you a choice, Mariam—"

"Just call me Mars."

"I'm giving you a choice, Mars: join me and lead the five women I've gathered. I need someone powerful enough to neutralize the others if required."

"You said I have a choice; what's my other option?"

"Join your friend here, and we'll see just what happens when a voidwitch joins the Legion. The likelihood of you maintaining your abilities is extremely low," she says flatly, "so I'd rather not go that route."

"You call that a choice?"

"I'm hoping you won't force my hand."

"What would I do, if I worked for you?"

"Mars, don't," Mookie says, sounding distant behind that thick glass. I shake my head subtly but don't look at him.

Hamid continues. "The six of you would be deployed as a commando unit. I would give you objectives, but how you carry them out would be up to you. This would only be two, perhaps three missions a year—you'd be brought in for situations that call for more nuance than the Legion is able to muster." I hear an edge of distaste to her voice when she mentions the Legion, but before I can press her, she continues. "You will be well paid, and in your downtime you can do as you like."

"I'd be a mercenary?" I say.

"Yes, I suppose."

"And my other option is to let you replace my skull and make me join the Legion?"

Hamid turns her android's hands so its palms face up. "What do you say?"

I rest my elbows on the table and hold my hands together in front of my mouth; pretend like I'm interested. I need to figure out how to disconnect Mookie before the nanotendrils, or whatever they are, get into his brain. I can't do that in here, especially not if they send Mookie to join the Legion.

"I'll get to leave Homan?"

"I can arrange for you to leave immediately."

"What about Mookie?"

"He will leave with you, of course. We still need to transfer him to a facility where the rest of the surgeries can be performed."

"Then I'm interested," I say, and Hamid smiles. "There's just one thing, though: if you're in charge of a fucking hive mind of cyborgs, why do you need me?"

Hamid shifts in her seat, and the chair creaks beneath the envoy as she does so. She purses her lips and rolls her head to one side. She sighs, then finally speaks, "The Legion is a hive mind, but I'm not its queen. I give them orders, but an amalgam of their minds decides how they respond to those orders. Most were military personnel before their transformation, or former military like your friend here. The one thing all those minds have in common is their military training—training that instills within them a fervent belief in the supremacy of the empire and the godlike status of the emperor."

I'm not sure I get it, so I say, "Why's that an issue?"

Hamid's hand rotates in its wrist cuff as she motions to me. "Your situation is a prime example. I should have been informed of your capture immediately; your fate should have been mine to decide. Instead, the Legion assessed your crimes and brought you here, and only informed me when you'd nearly arrived. They mistreated a valuable asset because they're unable to deviate from the letter of the law."

I chuckle. "You're recruiting witches because you've lost control of your toys? What happens if they catch you breaking the law one day?"

"I hope to never find out."

"How long until he's one of them?"

"It depends on proximity. I'll be in-system shortly; he should connect to the others quickly once I arrive with the Legion."

I keep my eyes on the commander. "Alright," I say. "I'll join you, but—"

"No!" Mookie yells, louder, pulling against the unmoving grip of Stockton's envoy. "Kill her and run!"

"You'd die, Mookie," I say, my voice wavering slightly.

"It's too late for me anyway."

I hold my eyes open wide and wait for the rising tears to dissipate. "I need to know something first," I tell Hamid. "Rathnam said my friends died leaving Miyuki; do you know if that's true?"

"I'm sorry, Mars," Hamid says, and my heart sinks. "I haven't heard anything about them."

Relief floods through my veins and I smile, shake my head, and exhale, all at once. "Okay," I say. "When do we leave?"

"I've ordered a shuttle up from Seward. It will take you down to the surface where you can meet the other five recruits and wait for me."

"They're already here?" I ask. *That might make things more difficult.*

"They were elsewhere when I dispatched the fleet to Seward, and they were not held up as I have been."

"How long 'til you arrive?"

"Under a day," she says.

I nod. Less than a day to ditch the space witches, contact the others—if they're still alive—and figure out how to disconnect Mookie from the Legion?

Plenty of time.

CHAPTER FIFTEEN

Rathnam bit his tongue when Hamid told him the news. I'm sure he was hoping I'd fight, so he could watch a robot cut my head open next. Even through the holo-unit I could see the disappointment in his eyes.

As Stockton leads me and Mookie to Induction for fresh clothing, he utters an endless litany of curses; muttering about how they shouldn't trust me, how they shouldn't let me go. *You're smarter than you look, fucko.*

Once I'm wearing clothes beneath my cloak, I hug Mookie, putting my arms high around his neck, above the bomb collar, so he has to bend down to my height.

Mookie whispers in my ear, "They told me you were all dead." He sniffs. "I'm glad I can hold you while I'm still me."

"Shut up," I say, then I squeeze him tighter, feeling how little of him there is to hold.

I make Stockton take us to the women's wing. Half of them stare at Mookie as we walk through the mess hall, eyes drawn to the first man they've seen, in the flesh, for the longest time.

Ali's at the far end with her back to me, hunched over and eating. I rush down the middle aisle between tables.

"Prisoner," Stockton bellows, but I ignore him—I'm no prisoner now.

I touch Ali on the shoulder and she turns, stands, and hugs me.

"Listen, I'm getting down to the planet," I say in Ali's ear.

I pull away and her eyes are wide. "You're leaving me?"

I hold her hand, and lean in close. "I'm going to get you out, but I need you ready, okay?"

She blinks slowly as she nods.

"I don't know how, but I'm going to shut security down. When that happens, I need you to get to the dock, and get everyone else to follow, okay?"

"Okay," she whispers.

"Prisoner!"

I squeeze her hand. "Goodbye, Ali."

• • •

At the tube station outside the Maximum Security Site, Stockton hands us over to another guard, then sneers and turns away. This second guard escorts me and Mookie through the transit system and brings us to the dock.

I pause to glance around the inside of the Sphere. It's

still breathtaking: incredible, beautiful, and weird. I haven't seen the farms, or gotten to explore the forest; I haven't discovered what kind of animals they introduced to create a biosphere. It feels like a missed opportunity, but that doesn't mean I want to stay.

"Your transport has arrived," the guard says. She lifts both hands like she's going to choke me, then I see the tips of her android fingers split open, revealing a set of fine tools. After a few seconds of work she pulls the collar away and stows it at her back. For the first time in weeks I can swallow without a dull pain at my throat.

She removes Mookie's collar too, and I put my hand on the back of his bare neck and feel the intricate scarring there. I pull his head toward me, and press my forehead to his. He's beaming.

"Your breath stinks," I say, and Mookie laughs.

The guard turns back to the tube, and within a couple of steps her head disappears. The gate over the dock tunnel grinds as it rises. One by one the lights along the tunnel floor come to life.

"Maybe I can be a medic in the Legion," Mookie says, "instead of a soldier."

I put my arm around Mookie's emaciated waist. "I'll figure something out, Mook; you'll never be one of those bastards."

Mookie hugs my shoulder and we walk toward the

dock's tunnel. "What are you going to do?"

"I'm not sure, but it'll be big."

I take one final look at the prison behind us, then we step into the tunnel, falling under the cold, void-black shadow.

CHAPTER SIXTEEN

As Mookie and I watch the movement of planetary bodies out the shuttle viewport, our two MEPHISTO min-
ders eyeball us, guns held across their laps. The local star
hides on the far side of Seward while the shuttle disen-
gages from Homan Sphere and takes us down toward the
planet's surface.

The capital city is a distant twinkling mass that slowly
takes shape as we approach. Street lights form concentric
rings joined by an axis of wider highways, the whole city
laid out like a gargantuan crosshair.

"It's huge," Mookie says, leaning his head on my shoulder as we watch the city coming into focus.

I nod. "I was just expecting a base."

The troopers look odd at the edge of my vision—real
faces, real skin, bodies that aren't uniform in size and
shape—flesh and blood instead of android steel. They're
standard grunts, lacking the scarring of the Legion, but
they still sneer at us like we're subhuman.

The shuttle keeps descending until we're close enough
to make out individual structures—towering skyscrapers

dwarfed by the barrels of two cannons reaching into the night sky. Near the center of the city, a column of solid light illuminates the surrounding buildings as it points to the firmament.

We come in low near this beacon, flying toward a huge ziggurat. The top of the building is stepped, with the highest floor jutting out like a squat head, and two more steps down before the rest of the building drops uniformly. There's a massive opening in its middle, and the shuttle's engines lower in pitch and spike in volume as we head into this central hangar.

The dock is vast, large enough for ships triple the size of our shuttle, and lined with dozens of vehicles. The largest of the space-faring vessels looks like it could hold a hundred passengers in a pinch; I'll need something bigger for the Homan breakout.

The shuttle lands with the gentle touch of an expert pilot, either human or AI, and the soldiers stand. They wait for me and Mookie to disembark first, playing it like the deferment is a courtesy. Really they just want to keep their weapons trained on our backs as we walk clear of the ship.

A man is waiting for us, young, attractive in a plain way, and dressed in a navy-blue suit. It has the sheen of fine spider silk, with the name "Ken" visible across the breast in shimmering threads of maroon.

He pretends to not notice the armed escort and says, "Mariam Xi, Cadwell Moreland, it's my honor to welcome you to the Hotel Benway." His is a clean, upper-class accent, from one of the planets in the Interior where Mandarin is spoken just as much as English.

Someone's a long way from home.

"Where are your bags?" Ken asks, with furrowed brows.

Mookie shakes his head. "We don't have any bags."

There's a pause, then Ken says, "In that case, please follow me."

. . .

It's a tight squeeze with five of us in the elevator car, but it's only a short ride to our floor. Walking the hotel corridors, the carpet feels lush beneath the thin soles of my prison shoes. It's patterned in maroon with large diamonds, intricately detailed with gold and indigo, and my feet sink with every step.

"Your accent's from the Interior, right?"

"You've got a good ear, Miss Xi."

"Spent a lot of time travelling, is all."

"What are you doing working here?" Mookie asks, and I can't help being surprised at his amicable tone. Starved, tortured, and skull taken apart in pieces, but he's still himself. *For now, anyway.*

Ken turns so he can look at us, but keeps walking, stepping backward. "I'm not sure what you mean; this is the finest hotel in all of New Tangier," he says, offering a polite smile.

"Kids from the Interior don't usually end up working service," Mookie says.

"Especially not at the ass-end of nowhere, beyond the empire's borders," I add.

Ken's eyes flicker to the soldiers walking behind me and Mookie. "I'm sorry, I can't really comment," he says, then turns to the front.

"These two don't care," I say.

"And you'll get no judgment from us," Mookie adds. "We just came from the Sphere; shit, we're still in our prison get-up."

Ken stops. His shoulders rise then fall in a sigh and he pivots back to face us. He speaks quietly. "I did some things I shouldn't have. My family is well connected, and if it were not for that fact, I too would be residing at Homan Sphere. This," he says, turning his hands out to encompass the hallway and the hotel and, well, *every-thing,* "was the compromise."

"Are there many like you?" I ask.

Ken turns and resumes leading us down the corridor. "I've met a few. Most of the workers on Seward, though, are here because it pays well."

"Gotta give people a reason to come all the way out here," Mookie says.

"I was just expecting a MEPHISTO installation."

"I think it started that way," Ken says, "but it expanded when the officers brought their families here. Having a civilian population leads to commerce, education, infrastructure. Here we are."

Ken stops at a door and presses his palm against a panel embedded into the cherry-tinted wood. The door beeps and Ken pushes it open then steps back from the threshold. "You should find everything you need in your suite; if not, please contact room service." Ken watches the guards as they take up positions on either side of the door, smiles at me, and departs.

I follow Mookie inside, half expecting the guards to push their way past us, but they wait in the corridor. The door closes with a blunt thud, and the voices coming from within the suite fall silent.

It's a wide room, walled on one side with floor-to-ceiling glass, showing the city skyline beyond. Lights glimmer all across the metropolis—streetlights, ship and nav lights, adverts, and a thousand other types. Above, the sky is a thick haze, glowing orange. The room is crowded with black leather couches around a squat coffee table. Five women sit, drinking red wine, pausing in their conversation to inspect me and Mookie.

I don't need to see their tattoos to know that these are the women Hamid was talking about. They have the same look as Briggs's voidwitch honor guard—disdain written in the set of their eyes and the curve of their lips; the certainty that they are special, powerful, feared. I'd probably have the same look on *my* face if I hadn't spent most of my life on the run, feeling hunted, alone, and vulnerable. Well, maybe not vulnerable, but definitely the first two.

I step forward, leaving Mookie behind me, and level a cool gaze at each of the women.

One of them stands. "You must be Mariam." She looks as though she's the youngest by at least a couple of years. Her skin is almost black in the dimly lit lounge, her hair in fine braids that coil and stack atop each other.

"Mars," I say. "And you are?"

She bows her head. "I'm Phoenix." She motions to the others and says, "This is Ortega, Minus, Anaya, and Lin."

Before I can speak, Ortega puts her glass down on the table and says, "You don't look like much." Her voice is deep and rough, like she gargles with booze and broken glass every morning. She's small but toned, with angular features and all-black eyes. There's an inch-thick line of emerald-colored hair down the middle of her scalp while the rest is shaved.

"And yet, I'm the one who killed Briggs, while you lap-dogs were ready to do his bidding."

Ortega sneers, but Phoenix speaks up again. "You really wiped out his whole operation?"

"Yes," I say, not taking my eyes off Ortega.

In my peripheral I see Phoenix's eyes go wide as she mouths something like "Wow." Lin nods appreciatively while the other two sip at their drinks.

Ortega walks over and stands close enough for me to smell the wine on her breath. "If you're so powerful, prove it."

Oh, I will. Not yet, but soon.

"I don't answer to you," I say. "I seem to recall Hamid putting *me* in charge of this little gang of turncoats."

"What did you say?" Anaya speaks through gritted teeth. She and the one called Minus get out of their seats and round the coffee table, coming right at me.

"Just say, how will you walk?" I say, and both Anaya and Minus stop dead in their tracks. The words are an echo of memory, carried across decades from our shared childhood to the now. In my own voice I hear the intonation of the caretakers that hypnotized us and planted these seeds of control. The other women have all gone static too, Lin with her glass tilted, burgundy wine dribbling over the edge and splashing onto her blouse.

"The man is dead, but you're still on his leash." I poke

Ortega's shoulder forcefully and she blinks and shakes her head. "Go sit down," I say, and she goes back to her seat, eyes tight with confusion, distrust, or both.

Anaya returns to the table and helps Lin mop up the spilled wine. Minus follows, sits down, and finishes her wine in one gulp. She doesn't speak.

"Do you trust Hamid?" I say to the room, not expecting an answer. "Do you think she doesn't already know about these hypnotic commands? Do you think she won't use them?"

Lin says, "How can you do that?"

"Listen," I say, ignoring the question, "we understand each other. We all went through the same shit when we were children. MEPHISTO has beaten and starved us, they've fucked with our bodies and minds. We're useful but expendable, and that's all we'll ever be.

"Take orders from Hamid, but don't trust her, and maybe—just *maybe*—one day we'll get out from under the empire's thumb, we'll be free."

• • •

"That was some speech," Mookie says, sitting on the edge of the bed, facing the window. "Isn't it dangerous to provoke them like that, though? There's five of them, and only one of you."

He takes some of the anti-inflammatories they gave him on Homan, as well as some painkillers. The swelling on his face has gone down, and I want to say he looks like himself, but his new eyes are off-putting in their unnecessary artificiality—silver sclera around the darker irises of the ocular lenses.

"When I found my sister she, uh, opened my mind. Those women aren't a threat." I exhale sharply. "I just hope I don't have to kill them when I turn on Hamid."

I'm sitting on the floor, leaning against the bed, glancing at Mookie's reflection in the glass. Even the bedrooms have a whole wall of window, that thin pane the only thing between us and the city, close enough to touch.

"You probably shouldn't talk like that," Mookie says. "The whole Legion might hear." There's quiet for a few moments while, outside, shuttle lights zip back and forth.

"We'll figure something out before it's too late; there's still time."

Mookie shakes his head. "Just, talk to me about the others; how were Trix and Squid when you saw them last?"

"Trix has been struggling," I say. I don't tell him it's because she feels guilty about wanting to leave him. "She blames me for what happened to you—rightly, I guess."

Mookie exhales loudly. "There was always a chance the authorities would find me."

I don't argue, but we all know that chance multiplied a hundredfold when I came along. "Squid's okay," I say. "They held everything together for the rest of us."

"Like they always do," Mookie says with affection. He lies back on the bed, still dressed, and within a few seconds he's snoring.

My implants haven't been properly disabled in years, so it takes some prodding for me to find the subdermal reset switches—one behind my ear, the other along my jaw. I press them both down and count three full seconds, then my HUD comes to life with diagnostic text scrolling too fast for me to read.

I lean my head back against the mattress and close my eyes, flickering orange text imprinted on the back of my eyelids. My leg jolts and I sit forward, forcing my eyes wide. I can't sleep, not yet. As soon as the reset is finished I can contact Squid and the others. Then I can sleep, only then.

• • •

I wake lying curled up on the floor, my head resting on my arm. After sleeping on hard polycrete, the carpet feels as soft as any bed I've ever slept in.

"Fuck." *I can't believe I let myself fall asleep.*

I sit up and wait for my eyes to adjust to the rich dawn

light. The sun peeks over the horizon and New Tangier looks distilled, hyper-real. The sky is a gradient of light blue through to the darkest gray. Homan glides across that expanse of void; it looks peaceful in its slow meander, but it's speeding through space—a hollow hell for the poor fucks we left behind.

A small icon blinks in the corner of my vision: a new message. I open it and it's just one word: *Ping*.

I check the message info and see it's a direct burst, meaning it came from in-system. My first thought is that it's Hamid keeping tabs on me somehow, but then I see hundreds more waiting for me, all saying *Ping*, all time-stamped an hour apart, going back weeks.

I burst back, *Waren?* and wait. A vox request appears in response.

When I open it, the line is dirty and there's a few seconds of static before Waren says, "It's about time. Do you have any concept of how boring this system is?"

I make a sound somewhere between a laugh and a sob, then I get up and jump on the bed. I grab Mookie by the shoulder and shake. "Mookie!"

He opens his eyes and peers at me, quizzical. "Wha?"

"Ignore the AI, Mariam," Squid says. "Do you have him? Do you have Mookie?"

"Yes, I've got him." Mookie sits up and I grab both his arms and say, "It's Squid and the others."

Mookie bursts out crying-laughing, grin stretched across his face and tears running down his cheeks. Tears well in my eyes too, and I rest my hand gently on the side of his head with my thumb curled around his ear.

"How is he doing?" Squid asks.

Mookie pulls away from me. He gets out of bed and stands, hugging himself.

"It's bad, Squid, really bad."

Mookie glances at me, and wipes his eyes with a knuckle.

"What did they do to him?" Trix comes on the line and spits out her question like it's an order.

"They make Legionnaires at the prison," I say. "He's—"

Trix makes an anguished sound and cuts me off. "You lost him."

I look over at Mookie, standing in the corner, running a hand over his bald, scarred head.

"I'll get him back," I snap.

"How?"

"He's alive, Trix, that's all that matters," Squid says.

There's a few seconds of noisy silence on the line. "They have to die," Trix says, cold. "The doctors, the guards, everyone that did that to him."

Including me?

"I need to be there. I need to help," she says.

"Later, Trix. Squid, are you close by?" I ask.

"As near as Waren can get without their scanners picking us up."

"Can you get long-range images of New Tangier?"

"Waren's already done it," Squid replies. "What do you need to know?"

CHAPTER SEVENTEEN

"There's no way you can do this," Mookie says.

I scoff, but the truth is, after all this time trying to tamp down on my power, some small part in the back of my head is worried I've lost it. "It'll be fine," I say.

Without anything else to do while he waited for me to get in touch, Waren drew up a dozen plans. He sent me heavily annotated orbital maps of Seward and Homan, long-range images of New Tangier analyzed and marked with points of interest, population centers, and garrisons. There were also pages of incomprehensible probability calculations that Waren was especially proud of.

I only had one question for him: *Which plan kept the others safest?*

"What do you need me to do?" Mookie asks.

"Just stay away from the window."

On the outskirts of New Tangier, the two massive cannons slice into the sky—effigies to man's lust for firepower. The towers are gunmetal gray, split into segments embossed with simple but striking designs; I guess if you're going to mar the skyline with colossal weapons, you've at least got to make them visually appealing. According to Waren, they're powerful enough to shatter any ship that approaches Homan; possibly they could destroy the Sphere itself.

I reach my hands out and breathe; my thoughts grow and swell, stretch out beyond the confines of my skull. I grab hold of the cannons and a quiet growl builds in the back of my throat as I start to tear the weapons down. The foundations crack, sharp thrum rising through steel—a vibration I can hear inside my head.

"Void-damn," Mookie says in a near-whisper, voice reverent.

Dust and debris erupt around the base of each cannon as they begin their inexorable fall to earth. Gravity takes hold, and the cannons become lighter in my grip. I shift them, angling their long stretches of metal to block off the expansive starport at the north of the city. It's empty now, but no doubt Hamid's armada will fill the whole space when she arrives.

I let go and the towers fall in slow-motion, bending against the force before they strike the ground, smashing office towers, apartment blocks, and barracks. Bits of detritus tumble to the ground like meteors.

My mind sings, glows; this is how it's supposed to be. I was made for this. I spent so many years fleeing systems of control when I was meant to be breaking them apart.

"I don't believe it."

I spin around and Phoenix is standing in the doorway. I grab her by the throat and yank her toward me, her feet off the floor as she crosses the room. I slam the door shut with my other hand and hold Phoenix in front of me.

"Mars, don't do it," Mookie says.

Phoenix groans, coughs. She croaks, "I want to help."

I drop her to the ground and she doubles over to catch her breath. Mookie puts a hand on her back and holds her wrist gently. He looks to me, checking I'm not about to hurt her again.

"What do you mean, 'help'?" I say.

"I'd been planning to break away from Hamid's witch squad the first chance I got." Phoenix wheezes. "I just figured I'd have to wait longer than this."

"Go then," I say, "this is your chance."

"But I can help you," she says again. Looking up at me, she could be the little sister I never had . . . if you replaced familial resemblance with a shared, fucked-up childhood, and manifest psychic abilities.

"You want to be free for once in your life?" I ask, and Phoenix nods. "Then go live whatever life you want for yourself."

Phoenix puts a hand to her throat and, with help from Mookie, stands up straight. She walks to the door and pauses, but then leaves.

"We could have used her," Mookie says.

"But could we trust her?"

"We trusted you," he says, softly.

I step away from Mookie and open a comm-link to Squid. "The cannons are down."

"I'm headed for Homan now," Squid says.

"Cut through the air lock, but don't leave the ship until you get word."

"I remember," they say: "autoturrets at the dock. Trix is coming for you in the shuttle. She'll be there in approximately six minutes."

"That's not part of the plan," I growl.

"Waren said the same thing. Good luck, Mars."

"Thanks, Squid. Voidspeed," I say, signing off. "Come on, let's go."

Mookie and I get out into the lounge area of the suite and the other space witches are standing at the window, watching parts of the city disappear in a cloud of detritus.

Ortega spins when she hears us. "This was you?" she asks, but her tone tells me she doesn't believe it. "Kill her," she says.

Ortega's already lashing out with her mind, but before the other women can strike, I push her assault aside and hit them all with a telekinetic blast. It shatters the window behind them, and the four witches tumble out the opening in a storm of glinting glass shards.

I walk to the edge and smell the acrid air of the city as a warm breeze rustles my cloak. We're too high up to see the ground, hidden by shadows, overpasses, and a drifting fog of dust. Already the women are little more than tiny dots falling out of sight toward the bustling streets below.

Mookie stands beside me with his hand closed above his sternum, looking down. He doesn't speak.

"If they're any good, they'll be able to break their fall," I say. I grab him by the arm to pull him back from the edge, but he shrugs my hand off.

I head for the exit, but it's sealed tight. I snap it off its hinges with a hard jolt and the metal door flies into the wall opposite.

The guards in the hall have their weapons up, but shock blanks their faces and slows their reactions. I lash out and a spray of crimson joins the rich colors of the carpet.

I glance back and Mookie is still standing near the broken window. "Mookie!" I call out.

His hand shifts from his chest to his head, and he pitches forward. I grab him before he falls over the edge and pull him back from the opening.

I cross the room and Mookie drops to the floor. He sits with both hands on his head, rocking slightly.

"What is it?" I ask, but I already know.

"They're in my head," he says in a slow, low-pitched drone.

The Legion is coming.

"We need to get moving," I say; "we need to stick to the plan."

I help Mookie to his feet and his arm shakes and spasms in my grip as I steer him out of the suite.

CHAPTER EIGHTEEN

We reach the hotel's hangar just as the *Nova*'s shuttle comes in to dock, landing gears resting on the ground with a soft thud.

The side hatch opens and Trix emerges, broad frame blocking the doorway, lasrifle in her hands and Ocho perched on her shoulder.

Trix walks down the steps and Mookie breaks away from me, stumbling forward, one hand on his head, the other reaching for Trix. He puts an arm around her as Ocho jumps clear and trots over to me.

"What's wrong with him?" Trix says, holding Mookie tight.

"It's started: his mind's being joined up to the rest of the Legion."

Ocho trills as she approaches then stands at my feet staring up at me. I get down on my haunches and she *maow*s, rubbing her chin on my knee.

"I know, little one; I'm sorry." She jumps on my lap and I grab her, hold her to my shoulder, and stand. I scratch the back of her head and she purrs. "I missed you too, jerkface."

"How do we stop it?" Trix asks. She seems pained, with fine wrinkles gathered around her eyes and her lips drawn down.

"I don't know, Trix. I don't know how they communicate, I don't—I don't even know if we can."

They break off the hug, but Mookie stands holding Trix, head resting on her shoulder. He groans loudly then stops.

"You said you'd fix him," she spits.

"I will," I say. "But right now we're wasting time."

. . .

I let Waren fly, but join him in the shuttle's cockpit, leaning forward in the seat because Ocho's asleep in the hood of my cloak.

"Can this thing go any faster?" I ask Waren.

"It's only a shuttle," the AI says, voice right inside my head. "Perhaps if you hadn't *crashed* my ship, we'd be able to get there sooner."

"You missed me, I can tell," I say, teasing.

"I miss my ship," he says.

"Yeah, well, I'll find you another one; I promise."

In daylight, I can see that the spire of light in the center of New Tangier is actually the communications tower atop the Homan Security Command Center. The pylon is snaked with cables and dotted with box antennae, relay dishes, and optic data ports. Waren says it's the link between the security command center and Homan Sphere: it's how they ride the envoys and control the power-shields; it's how they torture, beat, kill, or transform the prisoners they hold indefinitely.

Waren is sure I can tear the tower down and sever their connection with the Sphere, but I can't take the chance that they have backup systems in place.

He says it's time we can't afford to waste, but I need to deal with Rathnam personally. I'm going into the command center to rip it apart from the inside.

We dodge through the heavy traffic that careens across the sky as people rush to evacuate, plumes of debris rolling down city streets like waves. Military units converge near the fallen cannons, but if they're looking for what did this, they aren't expecting to find it riding shotgun in a nondescript shuttle.

Waren brings us in low, and we land on the eastern side of the Security Center rooftop, next to the comms tower. Sunlight falls through the metal structure in shafts, shadows crisscrossing the roof and wrapping around the shuttle.

"I'm going back to see the others," I tell Waren, then I unclip myself from the pilot's seat.

I hit the button beside the cockpit door and Waren says, "Things *do* tend to be less boring when you're around."

I smile. "See? You missed me."

Trix and Mookie are in the passenger hold, strapped in tight. Mookie is doubled over and Trix rests her hand on his back.

I crouch down in front of him. "Are you alright?"

He makes a sound like a low howl and the hairs on my neck stand up. "So many voices," he says. "So many . . . people . . . in my head." He snaps back, sitting straight up, hands going to the buckles of his seat belt. "I need to go. They need me. *We* need me."

"Strap him down, Trix, quickly." I reach for the storage container beneath the seats and toss her a length of poly-plastic tether.

She works quickly, restraining his arms by his sides, while I bind his legs together.

"I'm going into the Command Center. Stay here with Mookie," I tell Trix. "Waren—if things get dicey, take off, but keep close."

"I'm coming with you," Trix says, taking her lasrifle from the overhead rack.

"The Legion will be here soon," I say. "You need to stay and keep Mookie safe."

"He's not going anywhere, and I have to kill the bastards that did this to him," she says.

I know she feels guilty, I know that violence is the only solution she understands—fuck, if *anyone* gets that, it's me—but I shake my head. "If we lose him now, we might never get him back."

I hit the controls to open the shuttle door, and the ramp whines as it extends.

"We should have let you die in that ship," she says. "If Squid listened to me, we would have."

Her barb is a sharp pain in my chest; the truth of it hurts the most—they *should* have left me to die, their lives would be so much easier if they had.

I don't respond, I can't.

Trix stands, and before I can tell her again to stay, she says, "I'll take a defensive position on the roof, stop them getting near him."

"Fine," I say, because there's no arguing with her. We step out onto the rooftop. Surveying the skyline, the city looks still, but emergency service sirens drift in the distance. The noise brings Ocho out of my hood, to perch on my shoulder and take in the scene. She makes a curious-sounding trill and disappears back into the relative safety of my cloak.

"Waren, have you picked up the Legion fleet yet?"

The AI's voice sounds in my head: "Scanners onboard the *Nova* have detected a large fleet approaching Seward."

"They're coming here, not heading for Homan?"

"Correct."

"Good. Okay. Make sure Squid knows they don't have to free every single prisoner, not if it means putting themself at risk."

"You could open a link to Squid and tell them yourself," Waren says, "but no, don't bother; I'm an unnaturally intelligent being, surely I won't mind acting as a messenger daemon."

I ignore Waren and focus my attention on the skies overhead. I jack up the zoom on my ocular lens and scan across that expansive blue, cluttered with the distant shapes of MEPHISTO ships. At first they're just gray shadows, then the vessels disappear behind a burning glow as they hit the atmosphere.

The only ship that doesn't start to burn is the largest—Hamid's flagship, waiting in orbit.

The quickest ships—the fighters and corvettes—have already stopped burning, and their contrails dissipate into the air. I raise my hands and grab them one at a time, crushing the craft and dropping each mangled wreck as I reach for the next. I destroy twenty, thirty, more maybe, but still the sky is filled with MEPHISTO vessels.

"Go, Mars! I'll guard the ship."

I glance over at Trix. She's standing by the shuttle, lasrifle aimed at all that approaching doom, plugged into the shuttle's power for overcharge.

I rake the air with my thoughts one more time, catching a score of ships so they tumble, plunging out of sight and into buildings. They explode as they hit, distant booms echoing across the city, dopplering off the faces of skyscrapers.

I reach the rooftop access door and glance back at Trix one last time.

I hope you find whatever peace you need from this fight, Trix. Fuck knows it's going to be a big one.

CHAPTER NINETEEN

The building thrums with agitated energy, workers rushing down hallways, in and out of offices seemingly at random. In the commotion no one notices a space witch stalking the halls. Normally this would be a good thing, but I've got a whole building to explore and little time to do it.

I snake my thoughts out and grab someone at random. He yells in surprise as I drag him toward me, but he falls silent when we're face-to-face. He's a skinny, long-haired admin drone with the MEPHISTO insignia tattooed beneath his left eye.

"Where are the prison staff?"

"They're on the twelfth floor," he shrieks.

• • •

I take the stairs, and my calves are burning when I reach the twelfth floor lobby. The Homan staff must all still be working despite the chaos outside, because it's quiet down here—serene, if you ignore the noise from the omnipresent siren.

A security desk sits abandoned beside a reinforced entry marked with twelve in Roman numerals. I twist the blast door open slowly, metal creaking as I wrench it away, then drop it to the floor as quietly as I can. I walk through, taking in the space before me. I'm on a walkway about ten meters off the floor, overlooking a crowded pit lined with holo-rigs. They're clumped together in groups of four with thin access corridors between. Dozens of staff are illuminated by the soft green glow coming from their holo-consoles. I can't see their faces, hidden inside the shiny black rings of the apparatus, but I see their shoulders, watch their hands moving smoothly across the controls.

I'm finally here, in the detached heart of the prison, and it's so fucking mundane. All the pain of Homan Sphere originates in a dull room filled with the low hum of electronics and the artificial smell of filtered air. On Homan these people are abusers, torturers, and murderers, but down here? They're just boring fucking assholes, with a job, maybe a family, and either no conscience or a convenient series of lies they tell themselves to get through the day. I didn't want to think that evil could be so boring, so *normal*, but here it is, laid out in front of me.

They think just because the prisoners are a couple of hundred kilometers away, their hands are clean. They think just because these people are criminals they can treat them like they're less than human.

"Silence that alarm." *Rathnam.* His voice amplified over the blare of the sirens, just as digitized as I remember.

Hearing him speak, my heart beats faster, and my body must go tense, because Ocho climbs out of my hood and onto my shoulder. Her eyes are wide open, with her pupils in slits sharp as her claws.

Ocho lets out a low growl. "Soon, little face," I whisper.

I can't see Rathnam past the mass of cables hanging from the ceiling, so I creep farther along the platform. I get him in sight just as the alarm goes quiet. It keeps wailing in the distance, filling the rest of the building, but in here the only sound is Rathnam's yelling.

"You will remain at your posts and carry out your assigned tasks. Whatever is happening outside is none of our concern."

Don't be so sure, doc.

"But what about our families?" a voice asks.

Rathnam continues ranting at his staff, but I tune it out.

"Think we should kill him?" I ask Ocho.

She lets out a long *mraow.* I smirk, but my mouth goes flat when she leaps from my shoulder. She clears the walkway's safety rail then extends her glide membrane.

"What are you—" I hiss, but stop before anyone hears.

I move toward the stairs at the far end of the walkway, keeping an eye on Ocho as I go. She glides clean through the air, around the tangle of cables, and lands on the ring of a holo-rig. "Fuck," I say, under my breath, watching her jump from one rig to the next, tracking the sound of Rathnam's voice.

I sneak ahead as fast as I can without letting my footfalls clang on the metal platform. I hit the stairs right as I hear Ocho yelling and hissing. I rush down around the tight *U* of the stairwell to reach the ground floor.

"Whose animal is this?" Rathnam's voice booms, still amplified. He's on a raised platform, holding Ocho by the scruff of her neck. She keeps hissing, clawing at the air, trying to add to the bloody scratches she already put across his face. *Good girl.*

At first, only some of the staff raise their holo-rigs to see what's happening, but more of them lift the bulky equipment from their heads as a murmur ripples through the clusters: "It's her."

"She's mine," I say. Rathnam sees me now, and his mouth falls open.

One of the workers gets up from her seat and moves to intercept me as I stalk the aisle toward Rathnam. I toss her aside, high enough that she hits the upper catwalk with a clang and then tumbles to the ground, setting off a chorus of cries from the room.

Rathnam drops Ocho, and she meets me at the base of his platform. As I mount the steps, she climbs up to my shoulder and stands rigid, ready to keep fighting.

"Why are you here?" he asks. "You've been freed."

"Freedom's a funny thing," I say. "It's hard to enjoy when the people who hurt you are still out there."

He says something, but I can't understand it through his blubbering. *Not so fierce and commanding now, are you, doc?*

"Where's Stockton?"

"I'm here," a voice responds, defiant. I can't see his eyes in the shadow of his cap's visor, but I recognize the set of his jaw, twisted off-center in contemplation or anger.

I reach out and wrap my mind around Stockton's head; when I clench my fist his skull disappears with a sharp crack. Blood squirts into the air then falls, splashing Stockton's coworkers. *And you thought you could keep the blood off your hands.*

There are a few seconds of stunned silence before the screaming starts. Some bolt for the stairs, others stay at their consoles, too shocked or scared to move.

"What are you going to do," Rathnam says, "kill everyone here?" He says it quietly, but his mic picks it up and relays it to the whole room, amplifying chaos.

Seeing the staff panicked, screaming and crying—evil

rendered impotent—I should probably feel sorry for them. But even if most of them never touched *me*, they're all someone else's abuser—someone's Stockton, someone's Rathnam.

"You know what? That sounds like a great idea." I ball my hands as I bring them up beside my head, then make a guttural sound as I punch out. I carve through each row of staff, tearing apart guards and doctors, blood and body parts flung into the air. Lights flicker and equipment sparks, and the curtain of cables hangs loose from the ceiling, disconnected, swaying above the carnage.

Ocho jumps from my shoulder as I turn to face Rathnam—face pale as he surveys the display of gore. "You should have listened, doc: you should have left him out of it."

Rathnam holds my gaze for a moment, then keels over and vomits on the floor, spattering his expensive-looking brogues with congealed yellowish muck. He collapses, his knees landing in the puddle of sick. "What was I meant to do? He was my prisoner."

"Prisoners don't deserve to be treated like *people*?"

He shakes his head, but he isn't arguing, he's giving up.

"I won't let you die on your knees, doc."

He sobs when I lift him but stays silent for the rest. I carry him over to the dangling cables and wrap one around his neck. I let him fall, and he chokes as he kicks and struggles, his death throes booming from the speakers hidden in the ceiling.

I sit down at his command console. I find the turret controls and disable the weapons, then send Squid a burst to let them know. Next I find the controls for the powershields and switch all of them off. I hit a panel and bring the ring of the holo-rig down around my head. It takes me a few goes to trigger the mass broadcast, then suddenly my full field of vision splits into hundreds of tiny windows—each one showing a different envoy's POV.

"Listen up," I say, watching the images of all the prisoners turn to face the envoys I'm riding. "You're free to go. Head to the docks, there's a ship waiting."

I loop the message then start evacuation procedures, selecting the option to have the envoys remove collars as they shuffle prisoners toward the dock. When I get up from the console, Rathnam has stopped fighting, but his body still sways.

I make a kiss sound and Ocho rushes to me, the fur of her paws soaked in blood.

She runs up my cloak and deposits herself on my shoulder. "You are disgusting," I say, but she doesn't seem to mind. She just starts cleaning herself as I head for the exit.

CHAPTER TWENTY

"Where the hell are you?" Trix's yell cuts across my comms. In the background I hear ship engines streaking past and the whine of her lasrifle. "It's all gone to—"

Trix gets cut off, but I say, "I'm coming," in case she can still hear me. I try the elevator, and the building must have emptied out while I was busy with Rathnam, because it arrives within a few seconds. I hit the button for the rooftop, and once the elevator doors have closed I open a line to Squid. "How's the evac going?"

"The quarters and mess hall are packed tight; cargo hold is about half-full. I don't think they'll all fit, Mars."

"Just get as many as you can. How's Pale?"

"Sedated," Squid says.

"Good. No telling how he'd respond to all those people. I'm almost back at the shuttle, so we'll be with you in a few minutes." The elevator *dings* and the doors open. "Fuck," I say.

"Mars, what's—"

I cut Squid off and step out onto the rooftop. A MEPHISTO personnel frigate sits beside the *Nova*'s shuttle, with a line of thirty Legionnaires standing before both ships. The air overhead buzzes with countless craft.

Trix is on her knees in front of this formation with her hands linked behind her head. Mookie stands beside her, back rigid, face impassive, pointing a large, snub-nosed waver pistol at Trix's temple.

"Mookie," I call out, "this isn't you!"

"That's exactly right: it isn't him." A figure emerges from the MEPHISTO ship, and though I've only seen her via holo, I can tell it's Hamid. She wears a gray trench coat over her uniform, which flaps noisily as a cold wind crosses the rooftop. She stops next to Mookie and turns to face me. "Did you really think you'd get away with crossing me, Mars?"

I scoff, but I doubt she can hear it. The Legionnaires level their carbines, tracking me as I walk toward Hamid. I force a smirk. "To be fair, I never thought we'd actually meet."

The port to the north is lined with a dozen cruisers and twice as many frigates. Legionnaires move in perfect formation—visible even from here, like insects working to a common goal—unloading the ships and marching away from the landing. They fill the streets, great slabs of human machinery gliding across New Tangier, demonstrating the power of their queen.

Hamid's hair flows in the breeze, but she stands per-

fectly still at parade rest. "What did you think would happen?" she asks.

"I thought I'd be gone already. I thought you'd be
smart enough to let me disappear."

One of the Legionnaires walks out of line and holds
an arm out, stopping me about five meters from Hamid,
Mookie, and Trix.

"Even if you'd escaped, Mars, you would have had to
abandon your friend. He's mine now; he will forever be
part of the Legion."

I look up at the sky and see Homan drifting slowly
overhead. Hamid glances up too. "My flagship is moving
to intercept your other friends," she says.

I keep staring upward and send Squid a burst: *You need
to leave Homan, now.*

They respond: *I can't be sure everyone's on board.*

"I could have given you a good life," Hamid says.

I cross my arms over my chest. "Good, maybe, but it
wouldn't have been my life."

"You're a fool. Do you think anyone gets the life they
want? Life is compromise. Now, because you were too
selfish to comply, your other friends are doomed to share
this one's fate," she says, resting a hand on Mookie's
shoulder. She keeps talking, and I hold her gaze but let
my eyes lose focus.

With my right hand tucked behind my arm, I flex my

fingers and stretch my thoughts out. My mind is endless, infinite, and Hamid's flagship is so close, close enough to touch. I ensnare the massive vessel in a psychic net and pull. It shudders in my grip, engines fighting my grasp, and I start to groan, quiet enough that Hamid doesn't hear over her continuing tirade.

The ship starts to stall and I feel its weight shift. The noise in my throat builds and Hamid walks closer.

I send another burst to Squid: *Go* now, *or you won't save anyone.*

"What is she doing?" Hamid asks.

At the same moment, three of the Legionnaires say in unison, "Commander," and point to the sky. The flagship is sinking low enough that flames erupt around its edges as it dips into the atmosphere.

Hamid spins to face Mookie, his gun still pointed at Trix. "Shoot her!"

With my mind on the ship, I can't react fast enough, but Trix can. She pushes up from her knees, ramming Mookie hard in the stomach. He tumbles backward and the waver discharges as he hits the ground, the shot going wide.

Lying on his back, Mookie aims at Trix again. With wrists still cuffed, she shields her face and chest with her arms. Mookie shoots low. The gun squeals, then there's a sharp squelch and a fist-sized hole in Trix's gut.

I let go of the flagship and scream. Trix collapses forward onto her side and presses her forearm against the wound. Blood quickly pools around her. Too much blood, seeping from the open maw of flesh.

Mookie stands. He doesn't even look at Trix. Instead he rejoins the line of Legionnaires, waiting for their next order.

Hamid watches calmly as Trix bleeds out on the ground. "All of your friends will die, Mars. Either for me, or by my command. You never should have crossed me."

"Cross you? You're *nothing*." I spit the words out and lift Hamid into the air, feeling the weight of her steel skeleton. *That won't save you.*

"Kill her," she screams, but she needn't have bothered. Already the Legion is flowing toward me, thirty bodies moving for one purpose.

I hold Hamid tight, feel her in my mind like an insect trapped in a web—a dull presence I can't fully ignore as I tear the weapons from the hands and holsters of each Legionnaire. Mookie moves with the pack as they swarm closer, but I tear a length of cable free from the communications tower and wrap it tight around him. He falls to the ground, writhing.

By the time I'm done with Mookie, the nearest Legionnaires are close enough to grab at my clothes. Ocho jumps with claws out, landing on a Legionnaire's face and scratching deep cuts through geometric scars.

She's fast, but I'm faster; my thoughts are quicksilver. My eyes flash from one target to the next as I grab and crush, fling, throw, or tear reinforced skeletons apart. They drop, but the hive mind drives them on, arms reach from broken torsos to clutch at my ankles and at the hem of my cloak.

"Enough!" I yell, then I stomp the ground around me, crushing the fallen Legionnaires into the rooftop, the building vibrating under my feet, trembling like an earthquake just struck. I push my arms out hard, sweeping the rest of them aside and off the edge of the building. I watch them fall, bodies relaxed as gravity pulls them toward their doom. None of them scream as they drop.

Down in the streets, the marching Legionnaires are running now; I watch formations break as pieces of the hive scatter. A wave of them hits the building beneath me—some rushing inside, others scaling the walls, ascending on the strength of their unnatural bodies as gunfire fills the air over my head.

"Let me go," Hamid says, breathlessly, still caught tight in my grip.

I ignore her plea and rush over to Trix. Her breathing is ragged, face unnaturally white, clothing caked in gore. She looks at me, eyes clear and focused even as blood seeps from her lips.

"Promise me you'll save him," Trix croaks. She starts to say more, but her voice cracks and she goes silent.

Mookie is a few meters away, rolling on the ground, still struggling against the makeshift restraints. His face is a calm mask—there's no hatred or anger in his eyes, only duty. He's Legion, through and through.

We lost him to Homan Sphere but I got him back—I can get him back from the Legion too. I just need to—

"They'll never stop," Hamid says. "They won't stop until you're dead."

"You're right," I say to Hamid, loud enough that she can hear me over the din of distant chaos. "They won't stop, unless I stop them."

Homan Sphere.

The prison drifts placidly across the sky. It looks so peaceful at this distance. Hamid's flagship has righted itself, and every engine on its bow glows bright as starshine as it pulls out of Seward's gravity well. I ignore the flagship and reach out farther. I lift my hands up into the air, and with my fingers spread wide I grab hold of Homan Sphere. I feel its mass like a stone in the center of my brain. I skip the quiet noises and go straight to screaming as I reach out with every piece of myself. My heart thuds hard, so hard my chest rocks and my body sways, but I feel Homan go still: it stops spinning, stops its inexorable orbit.

I fall silent and exhale slowly; my body shakes, but I'm calm. This will only work if I'm calm, focused. My throat is raw, and my vision is blurred with tears. I can't tell if it's working, so I hold my eyelids open until the film of liquid clears, until I see the moon growing larger by degrees.

"What are you doing?" Hamid yells, incredulously. She's loose now, forgotten when I grabbed Homan. I forget her again.

I keep pulling. I fall to my knees but barely notice. My neck aches, my arms flood with pain, but I keep offering them to the sky. Homan looms large. I inhale and scream again as I pull. Gravity shifts, Homan falling on its own; Seward itself is pulling with me.

I collapse forward onto my hands and I pant and force myself to breathe. Ocho rubs herself against my arm, but I can't speak. I pick her up and hold her to my chest as I stand.

I step over scattered pieces of Legionnaires as the sky itself starts to rumble. I pick Mookie up and lift Trix out of the pool of her blood. A sharp pain stabs through my brain as I carry them to the shuttle; I wince, and push through it.

"What have you done?" Hamid grabs my arm and spins me to face her.

I shake her off and knee her in the stomach. She doubles over and stumbles back. "Stay here and die with your precious fucking Legion."

I get the others onboard and Waren takes off without a word. Legionnaires reach the rooftop, crowding in to protect their queen. *Too late.* Outside the viewport, the atmosphere starts to burn. Homan crashes into Hamid's flagship, shattering the vessel, and continues to fall slowly to the ground. Half the sky is fire.

The shuttle engines hit a pitch I've never heard them reach before as Waren boots up from Seward's surface. MEPHISTO vessels lift off from the port, and craft all over the city start to scatter. Most of them won't make it; they didn't have our head start.

We're high above New Tangier now, the city in Homan's shadow. We break atmosphere as the city disappears behind the hollow moon. Finally, with a thunderclap louder than death, it's gone.

Mookie stops fighting against his restraints and falls silent as Seward burns.

"Mookie?" I lean over him but he stares through me, eyes wide as he hyperventilates.

CHAPTER TWENTY-ONE

Seward is unrecognizable by the time we dock with the *Nova*; there's no city, no flagship, no fleet—no Legion.

Massive tsunamis roll across the planet, collide, coalesce, and then divide. They appear slow and gentle at this distance, but when one of them strikes the planet's sole continent it blasts through the smoking debris-packed crater where New Tangier used to be. Ragged remains of Homan's shell rock and tumble, like boats in a storm. Steam pours into the atmosphere in plumes where seawater floods into the planet's mantle, magma spewing from the colossal wounds like fiery blood.

Squid joins me at the viewport. They don't speak for what feels like a full minute. "We should go, before they send a fleet to see why Seward fell silent."

I nod, and my migraine peaks; I feel my head turn to the side, cold spear of pain through the right hemisphere of my brain. I haven't had a headache like this since Sera opened my mind with those encephallucinogenic mushrooms. I also haven't pulled a moon out of orbit before, shifting thousands of tons of steel and stone with nothing but my thoughts; of course the strain of that is going to hurt.

"I was thinking we'd go to Aylett Station," Squid says. "From there all the people we rescued can find work, transport home, or whatever else they might need."

"Sounds good," is all I can manage.

"I'll tell Einri. After that, we should talk."

They leave me, and after a few moments the view of Seward cuts away and the stars disappear as we enter worm-space. I stay at the viewport and stare into the abyss.

• • •

Ken walks backward down the hallway of the hotel. A wall of fire rages at the end of the corridor, flames roiling but silent. It moves toward us in slow motion.

"Stop," I say, but Ken keeps moving.

The flames engulf him.

I wake on my side with Ocho curled up at my chest, purring. I scratch her chin and she shifts in her sleep. I bring my legs up, fold myself around her, and try to nap.

• • •

"I don't see why we need to have this meeting," I say. Pale

is sitting on my lap, with Ocho asleep on *his* lap.

We're in the shuttle, docked with the *Nova* because the hold is crammed full of refugees, cut off from all our passengers while Einri flies us toward Aylett. The stench in the *Nova* is thick with humanity—sweat, sex, and other stinks. Ali was one of the first to reach the ship when Squid docked with Homan, a trail of prisoners following behind her. She's been telling them all that I saved them; she says I'm a hero, and some of the others agree.

Which is why I've been hiding out in the shuttle.

"Mars," Squid says softly, "you destroyed a whole city. You need to talk about that."

Pale turns around to look at me and his bony butt digs into my legs. I still don't know how much he understands, but the awestruck look on his face tells me that he might grasp "destroyed a whole city."

"How's Mookie doing?" I say, just to change the subject.

Squid sighs and leans forward in their seat. "He's not good. One moment he's catatonic, the next he's hysteric. Either way he won't leave Trix's side."

I nod. I haven't seen her body since I put her into storage in the medbay. Part of me wants to say goodbye, but that means facing Mookie, and I'm still not ready for that. Maybe I never will be.

"Mars," Squid says, "I won't judge you, but you need to

talk about what you did."

Maybe you should *judge me, Squid. Maybe I can't talk about it because I'm too busy judging myself.* "I just need some time alone," I say. "Once we unload everyone at Aylett and I get a new ship, I'll go, and I'll get my head together."

"We're here for you, Mars."

"But you shouldn't be," I say. *Unless you want to die too.*

"You've got about an hour until we reach Aylett," Squid says. They don't say it might be my last chance to see both Trix and Mookie, but the subtext is there in the gaps between words. "I'll be in the cockpit helping Einri with the docking procedures."

Squid lingers at the doorway for a moment before deciding to stay silent. They leave the shuttle; the burst of sound coming from the *Nova* dies abruptly when the door closes again.

• • •

Pale holds tight to my hand as I walk through the *Nova* to the medbay. Refugees step aside to let us squeeze pass, huddling together to whisper about me in hushed tones.

Mookie doesn't look up when Pale and I walk into the medbay. There's a subtle hint of putrefaction to the air, Trix's body laid out on one of the cold chamber drawers, pulled out from the wall. A white sheet covers her ruined stomach, but not her face or arms, and Mookie clutches her blue and lifeless hand.

"Pale wanted to see Trix," I say.

Mookie's arms are stippled in goose bumps, and he's shaking, but whether it's from grief or the cold, I can't tell.

Pale pulls me closer and we stand next to Trix's body, opposite Mookie. Pale stares at her and raises a hand as if to touch her shoulder, but then he pulls it away.

This wasn't part of the plan, Trix. You could have stayed on the Nova; *you didn't have to die like this.*

"Mookie, I—" *I don't know what to say.*

"You never should have come for me." He glances up and I see a flash of silver, but he doesn't quite meet my eyes before he looks back to Trix.

"You know we couldn't have done that. We had to find out what happened to you, we had to save you."

"You should have left me," Mookie says, louder. He groans and then smacks his forehead with the palm of his hand. "You should have died, you should have—"

He turns away from Trix and walks to the corner of the small room to lean his head against both walls. "You killed me—you killed them. You killed *all of us!*" He yells the last bit. "They were there, in my head; I knew them all, I knew them like I know myself, and you just fucking killed them. I was there when it happened; I died *thousands* of times. Now I'm alone, without them, without Trix; there is no one here, there is *nothing.*"

"The Legion killed Trix, Mook. I had to stop it. I—"

He spins back, face twisted in anguish, a stream of tears running down each cheek. "You're a fucking *monster*. Leave," he says, then he starts screaming, "leave me alone, leave me alone!"

Pale starts to cry, so I hold him tight and press his head into my stomach, hand covering his ears. I lead him out of the medbay with my arm around his shoulder, but pause in the doorway. "Sorry, Mookie." *I'm so fucking sorry.*

EPILOGUE

I sit cross-legged on a tall crate in the *Nova*'s hold, Ocho resting in my lap, cleaning herself. I smooth her fur with my hand, just to make her clean it again.

All the refugees have gathered around us, waiting for the large bay doors to open, swelling forward at intervals, impatient for the freedom we promised them. For some, it's a return home, for others it's a foreign station, full of as much threat as promise. At least they're safe now. There's no Legion left, no MEPHISTO to come looking for them.

A current moves through the crowd, and in snatches I see Mookie pushing a hover gurney toward the front. People begin to protest but fall silent when they see Trix's body; nobody wants to interrupt a funeral procession, no matter how small or informal.

With a hollow clang the bay opens up, pieces of steel pulling away, revealing the bustling dock of Aylett Station and carrying the smell of fern to my nose. I expect a rush, but all the former prisoners wait for Mookie to get clear first. Once he has disappeared into the motion of the hangar, they start to leave, slowly at first, but then I hear cries and laughter, and people begin to run.

I put my rebreather on to cut out the smell, then wait a few minutes until everyone has cleared out. I lift Ocho to my shoulder and drop down off the crate, following in the wake of the refugees, displaced and broken, but alive. They have that at least, more than Trix, more than the people of Seward.

By habit I head out of the dock, mentally planning my route down to the Ring One bar, but I pause when I remember that Miguel won't be there. Out of the corner of my eye I see a small stall set up in front of an old Blackcoat-class ship—maybe "stall" is too generous. It's a collection of tools, gear, clothing, and random tchotchkes laid out on a large, half-empty tank of water. The two women behind the tank smile brightly as I approach, and their daughter looks up from where she sits beside them.

"Ooh, kitty," she says excitedly.

I take Ocho from my shoulder and put her on the ground near the girl. She eyes the small human warily, but accepts the pats.

I'm not sure what people say to parents about their children, so I smile and say, "She's beautiful." Hearing my distorted voice through the rebreather, I pull it from my face.

"Do you have one of your own?"

I think of Pale, but shake my head. "What are you selling?"

"Everything. We just moved here, and our unit's a little smaller than we're used to."

I set aside two jumpsuits that are close enough to my size, then pick up a chunky bracelet carved with fine patterns. It won't let me pass through powershields, but it'll stop my wrist from feeling so naked. I set it on top of the clothing and ask, "How much for these, and the ship?"

"The ship?"

"If you're staying, you don't need it, right?"

The two confer, and I open a link to Waren, plugged into the *Nova* systems. "What do you think of Blackcoat-class ships?"

"Corvettes but built like small frigates. Plenty of space, lots of armor, but not particularly fast."

"Would you be happy to call one home?" I ask.

"Anything to get me away from Einri; that thing is terminally boring."

I watch their little girl play with Ocho, letting her long hair hang down and making it dance so Ocho leaps forward, claws slicing harmlessly between the fine strands.

When the women are done talking, I have to haggle them down a little, and they agree to throw in the bulky water jug for nothing. I hand them the cred chip Sera gave me—every credit left to my name—and they send a secure burst containing the ship's deed and access codes.

When we're done, the girl waves goodbye to Ocho, hardly even aware I was there.

I delve further into the Station to stretch my legs and clear my head, and I catch bits of imperial news. They can't say where Seward was, but they make it sound like it was a burgeoning beacon of civilization, not a planet that only existed to service a secret, illegal prison. They've dug up an old photo of me from one of my compromised fake IDs and they broadcast my name across the galaxy, blaming me for the "Slaughter at Seward."

I install Waren's core into the new ship, then return to the *Nova* to grab my scant belongings. Squid carries my bag to the ship, insisting they should help, when I know they just want to say goodbye. We hug, and they hold on a little too long.

"You'll let me know about Mookie?" I ask.

Squid nods. "Are you sure you won't stay?"

"I can't, Squid." Even if I weren't public enemy number one across hundreds of worlds, something horrible happens to everyone I get close to—everyone but Squid, so far.

"I'm worried about you, Mars. Promise you'll stay in touch."

"I promise," I say. "Where's Pale? I couldn't find him."

"He was napping."

"Tell him bye from me, okay? You'll take those files we found to a doctor and get his seizures sorted out?"

"Of course," Squid says. They hug me again, and say in my ear. "I will see you soon."

I pull Ocho from my hood and hold her out to Squid. Squid scratches her chin and kisses her on the head, but Ocho's never been one for goodbyes.

"Bye, Squid. Thanks for everything. And sorry."

I board the ship, and close the air lock doors behind me without turning for a final look.

I press Ocho to my shoulder and scratch the back of her head as I walk toward the cockpit. "I suppose we'll need a new name for this ship, won't we?" I ask, but Ocho only purrs. "Waren, feel free to take us out at your leisure."

The AI doesn't bother to respond, but the floor hums beneath my feet as the engines start warming up. I take the pilot seat and Ocho squirms out of my grip, drops to the floor, and scampers away.

Some time later, Waren intones, "We have reached minimum safe distance."

"How do you like the ship?" I ask.

"I suppose it will do," Waren says.

"Be glad you don't have a sense of smell; that family spent way too long cooped up in here."

"Whilst I may not have olfactory senses—and thanks for rubbing that in—I *have* detected something moving in Cargo Hold B."

"Probably just Ocho," I say, but then I swivel my seat and see her asleep in the corner of the cockpit. "Void-damn it."

The ship is dark, and my footfalls echo off the flat metal walls. I hit the button to open the hold, and there he is, eating one of my rations, with another two empty packets on the floor beside him.

"Pale, what are you doing?" I say.

The boy wipes his mouth with the back of his hand and smiles.

I sigh and crouch down to his height. "Waren, turn the ship around."

Pale says, "No," and shakes his head vigorously. He gets up and throws his sauce-covered hands around my neck.

"You want to stay with me?" I ask, and I can tell he nods because he digs his chin into my shoulder. "I'm sorry, kid, but it won't work."

He pulls back, then he pats his chest and then points at me. He repeats the movement a couple of times.

"You're saying we're the same?"

"Yes," he says, nodding.

"That's not a good thing. Waren?"

"There's no turning back, Mars."

"What do you mean?"

"You need to see this."

I stand and hold my hand out for Pale. "Come on, you stowaway."

We walk back to the cockpit and he sits down next to Ocho and pats her. She stretches and opens her eyes, but then closes them again and keeps sleeping. The ship's aft-view is up on the viewscreen. Aylett hangs just off-center, the void between us and it filled with three military carriers and a mass of frigates too distant to count.

Waren zooms in tight so we can see the imperial insignia adorning the hull of each carrier: the Janos stag beetle with wings spread wide. "It's the Emperor's Guard," Waren says, sounding oddly calm.

Fuck. My heart stops for a moment too long, then begins to race. The emperor's private military police force. It was supposed to be the end: Briggs killed, Hamid and the Legion dead on Seward, nothing left of MEPHISTO but scattered outposts. *I was meant to be free of all this.*

"They appear to be tracking us, Mars. What do you want me to do?"

"Just get us out of here." Looking at Pale I sigh. "I guess you're stuck with me."

He grins at that and I can't help smirking.

"Have you got a destination in mind?" Waren asks.

"Did you get a copy of the Miyuki records from Einri?"

"Of course; that glorified calculator wasn't even interested."

"Then we've got everything we need to treat Pale's medical condition, except a doctor. Punch in coordinates for Joon-ho—I know someone there we can trust."

Is this how it started for Squid? Take on one stray, and next thing you know you've got a small crew of people who need you? I'll have to start holding family meetings too. A space witch, an untethered AI, a broken psychic boy, and a self-cloning cat-thing: what a weird family.

An immense field of stars stretches out beyond the cockpit viewport. It's a view that feels like home. I didn't realize how much I'd missed it inside Homan, but staring out at these familiar constellations, something in my chest glows warm.

"Calculations complete; just say the word."

"First, tell Squid we had a stowaway and he's staying with us for the time being."

There's a pause, then Waren says, "Message away."

"Alright—get us out of here before they get any closer."

"When will you let *me* choose our destination?" Waren says.

"Next time, Waren, I promise."

The galaxy folds away and the stars vanish as we slip into a wormhole, leaving behind the wrath of the empire. We're fugitives, outside the law and beyond the walls of the universe. It's safe here, adrift in darkness. Too bad we can't stay.

ACKNOWLEDGMENTS

Special thanks to Bryony Milner for her all her support, feedback, and friendship. Phoenix belongs to you. Thanks also to Marlee Jane Ward, whose work is an inspiration and whose support is invaluable. And thanks to Austin Armatys for his feedback, support, and encouragement.

Thanks to Carl Engle-Laird for his support, his keen eye, and his editorial skill. Thanks also to the rest of the team at Tor.com Publishing for all their hard work.

I owe a debt of gratitude to both Chelsea Manning and Gregory Whitehead, whose work informed certain aspects of this book.

About the Author

Photograph by Marlee Jane Ward

COREY J. WHITE is a writer of science fiction, horror, and other, harder to define stories. He studied writing at Griffith University on the Gold Coast, and is now based in Melbourne, Australia.

Find him at coreyjwhite.com and on Twitter @cjwhite.

TOR·COM

Science fiction. Fantasy. The universe.

And related subjects.

*

More than just a publisher's website, *Tor.com*
is a venue for **original fiction, comics,** and
discussion of the entire field of SF and fantasy,
in all media and from all sources. Visit our site
today—and join the conversation yourself.